SEA, POISON

Caren Beilin

Sea, Poison

A NEW DIRECTIONS
PAPERBOOK ORIGINAL

Copyright © 2025 by Caren Beilin

All rights reserved.
Except for brief passages quoted in a newspaper, magazine, radio, television,
or website review, no part of this book may be reproduced in any form
or by any means, electronic or mechanical, including photocopying
and recording, or by any information storage and retrieval system,
or be used to train generative artificial intelligence (AI) technologies
or develop machine-learning language models,
without permission in writing from the Publisher.

This is a work of fiction. Characters, places, and events
come from the author's imagination, or are used fictitiously,
and any resemblance to actual people, places, or events is coincidental,
though gynecological crime is real.

An excerpt from this novel first appeared in *MsHeresies*.

Passages quoted from Shusaku Endo, *The Sea and Poison*, translated by Michael Gallagher
(New Directions, 1992). Used by permission. Lyrics from "Survivor" and "Brian's Song"
by the band Fifteen used by permission of Jeff Ott. Lyrics from "In Your Eyes"
written by Peter Gabriel. Courtesy of Real World Music Ltd. All rights reserved.
Lyrics from "Blue Chicago Moon" and "Almost Was Good Enough" written by Jason Molina,
published by Autumn Bird Songs (ASCAP) / Secretly Canadian Publishing (ASCAP).
Used by permission. Lyrics from "You Oughta Know" by Alanis Morissette.
Music by Alanis Morissette and Glen Ballard. Copyright © 1995 Songs of Universal, Inc.,
Vanhurst Place Music, and Arlovol Music. All rights for Vanhurst Place Music administered
by Songs of Universal, Inc. All rights for Arlovol Music administered
by Penny Farthing Music c/o Concord Music Publishing. All rights reserved.
Used by permission. Reprinted by permission of Hal Leonard LLC.

Manufactured in the United States of America
First published in 2025 as New Directions Paperbook 1649

Library of Congress Cataloging-in-Publication Data
Names: Beilin, Caren, author.
Title: Sea, poison / Caren Beilin.
Description: New York : A New Directions Paperbook Original, 2025.
Identifiers: LCCN 2025010277 | ISBN 9780811239516 (paperback) |
ISBN 9780811239523 (ebook)
Subjects: LCGFT: Novels.
Classification: LCC PS3602.E384 S43 2025 | DDC 813/.6 — dc23/eng/20250318
LC record available at https://lccn.loc.gov/2025010277

10 9 8 7 6 5 4 3 2 1

New Directions Books are published for James Laughlin
by New Directions Publishing Corporation
80 Eighth Avenue, New York 10011

Contents

Plaquenil   3
Methotrexate   23
Orencia   29
Naked Grapes   34
Xeljanz   40
Rinvoq   50
Fresh Prince   56
Carbon Balloon   68
A Manager   77
Those to Be Judged   97
Cooking Without Cumin   104
Fuck Chair   106
Why Would There Be a Uterus   111

Acknowledgments   115

SEA, POISON

Plaquenil

I'D NEEDED AN EYE EXAM SO TO SAFELY START TAKING hydroxychloroquine, which is a synthetic version of quinine if you remember *Heart of Darkness* and Kurtz's madness, him glugging the antimalarial, and behind him the skulls being used as fence caps. I wasn't going to the Congo. But for my autoimmune condition, hydroxychloroquine (Plaquenil) is usually prescribed as a first course of action.

Quinine is a naturally occurring material, found in a certain tree bark, while hydroxychloroquine — synthetic — only mimics its *quinoline*, its ring-system structure. Marketed and sold as Plaquenil, the drug might damage your ability to see color. Therefore, in order to begin, you need an eye exam.

I went, as my insurance — in 2018, through Obamacare — dictated, to the Moody Eye Clinic in Philadelphia, adjoined to one of the university hospital systems in this city of universities and their hospitals, or perhaps the other way around.

I've never worn glasses and was entirely new to the world of eye clinics, it was an extremely busy place. It most resembled the feeling of being in a busy bus terminal in Santiago, Chile, when I was 21 — now I was 35. It became clear the deal with this clinic is that you are there all day. People, most on the older side, were camped out in a dingy and enormous atrium, an enormous waiting *arena*, with numbered tickets withering in their palms.

That is what your appointment got you, I soon found out, an opportunity to be handed a ticket.

I sat there in a flimsy striped summer dress realizing I was hungry and freezing in the air conditioning, and my nipples were lengthening and hardening. I had not, even in my mid-thirties, reconciled myself to even a light foam padding in bras. Or bras really. I wore camisoles under clingy and short dresses. I hadn't been looking too deeply into many mirrors, with no professional job to keep me in that kind of line. I was working at an upscale corner grocery (a wall of dried, sugared fruits, kiwis, curling dried papayas, but specializing mostly in fish and wine, after all it was called Sea & Poison).

I was older than my coworkers, who were "rising seniors" and would stay for a year. I'd been there for about three years, having risen before (incompletely, I'm a dropout) at a Midwest arts college, then I had returned to Philadelphia — this city of hospitals — and worked for a decade at the Ritz, then changed over to Sea & Poison, I was a writer and I was writing. I didn't pluck my eyebrows or groom myself much beyond showering. It wasn't that I wasn't vain, I was. But I was more beautiful at this time. Not meaning because I was younger (again, 35) in 2018 than I am now — now I'm 41. More, my health has in recent years put my beauty on an unexpected chopping block. It's less linear than getting old. There are certain drugs — drugs beyond Plaquenil — I've taken that changed the texture of my hair, changed the image, a beautiful image, scratched the image. This was unexpected, that's all. These drugs have knocked something off center, have scratched at my face and hair. They have helped me enormously. I don't know what to say, I'm saying I have a cracked appearance.

It's not a pity party, it's a character sketch.

Insofar as you'll need to be looking at me, that your mind should fill me up with its own swaying cognitive and toxic reeds if we are to do this, your imagination should touch me with its ridiculous poison.

I'm sure I'm beautiful, in the way people are because they are standing, or how they are, the how-tilt about being, because of that notorious enough beauty of breathing and being. Because I am loved, because God loves me. Birth of July: to me, feeling hot is almost everything that's out there.

After a few hours in the waiting arena, at Moody, I was called up to get my baseline eye test. An ophthalmologist's assistant noticed I was reading Teju Cole's novel *Every Day Is for the Thief* (thank God I brought a book — at the time my phone being flip) and we talked about Cole's autofictional return to Nigeria, his hopes and disappointments about modern Nigeria, and she, the assistant, told me she had always suspected *she* was Nigerian, that her ancestors had been taken from Nigeria. She had always felt Nigerian, when she met other, certified Nigerians. I remember hoping in this conversation to affect attunement, and receptivity to her frankness, her openness — frankly, her chattiness — which after all is expected in Philadelphia, this city of hospitals, and, honestly, a city of chitchat. It helped that there was a big machine glommed onto my entire face, through which she studied only my eyes, only scientifically.

She called in the ophthalmologist, her boss, since she was done with her initial exam, and he thanked her quite gravely, because it turned out this whole time we'd been talking Teju she had been catching something troubling during the exam, a narrow angle I had in each of my eyes.

In an alarmed and commanding tone, this ophthalmologist — who seemed to be in his eighties and would remind anyone of the actor Max von Sydow — told me that I must go immediately to a new floor and wait there — particularly the Sydow of *The Exorcist* (1973), where the actor plays the older priest arriving to do the exorcism of the tween, Regan.

"I believe we should begin," Father Merrin (I am looking it up just now, watching a short YouTube clip) says upon arrival, to young Father Karras.

"Do you want to hear the background of the case first, Father?"
"Why?"

I was, this priestlike figure next explained to me at the Moody eye clinic, susceptible to a sudden blindness. He appeared to be panicked, *so* impatient, and he ushered me directly onto the elevator and he wished me well — gravely again, and sounding exceedingly alarmed, tired, he was old, but also busy, considering the waiting room, which I realized did not remind me of a backpacking trip to South America from my early twenties as much as Ellis Island, and he not Merrin from *The Exorcist* but an even older von Sydow of *Hannah and Her Sisters* (1986), where he acts as a cuck.

I invoked the genocide of Congolese people. I wrote at the start of my novel about Kurtz in *Heart of Darkness* using their skulls to decorate his fence posts, with these paper skulls that were once, if you unwrap the paper, and shred the frame (the literature), souls.

It makes me think of how there is no character sketch, no beginning of a book or anything, that genocide doesn't sway right into the insides of. From the start. No enunciation of a person, or a story about what happens with that person, that isn't already describing how we're offset by enormity. Big evil. To get to know a character I'm trying to say, is to look at me, a descendant of a different genocide altogether — dark, curly brown hair, brown eyes, slim — trait, trait, another trait — cracked — offset by piles of bodies or rivers of bodies, bodies made small by being multiplied by more murderers.

How does a person you are getting to know, someone in a novel, walk around or through these piles, and what kinds of sentences, as well, use their commas and dashes and more places inside of them, things like clauses, to show somehow and I don't know how the way the piles (of people) bulge, embolden, bloat and collapse the shape of sentences, but more, I think I wanted, when I began this novel, to try invoking a frame narrative, as *Heart of Darkness* is one of the most famous of these out there.

Why Sea? Why Poison? Is my place of work of so much importance to this writing? There is no actual sea in Philadelphia. Only a veritable sea of hospitals. The medical professionals in their blue and green scrubs aquamarize all of our city, at all hours. The flow of medicine, blood, and bedding. There's poison.

On a break from Sea & Poison, back in 2018, I skipped my lunch to do my blood draw at LabCorp, where patients from all the surrounding hospitals in Center City pooled into rows of metal chairs with their orders for different kinds of draws. We looked like actors on audition, nervous with our scripts. I had to give sixteen tubes of blood, which made me faint, but the technician who drew my blood wasn't allowed to give me anything to drink. Liability. I swallowed ferociously at myself, trying to drink from my own throat, with my head down, for about ten more minutes. The results, a week later, showed I *did* have the suspected autoimmune problem, accounting for the ways my fingers had swollen and stiffened, and the first thing would be to get the eye test, to be cleared to try hydroxychloroquine.

It's not quite quinine.

"Call Moody today, they are always so backed up for appointments."

By the time I had my appointment — my ticket — at the Moody Eye Clinic, I'd waited four months since I'd gotten those upsetting results. I'd been mercifully prescribed a course of Prednisone to take, to wait out my entry into a potentially longer-term treatment of Plaquenil. It seemed a shame, though, that I couldn't live on Prednisone. Within two days of starting it, my stiffened fingers could bend and were back to normal size. Before this miracle (of Prednisone, the steroid) I'd been walking around under the moon fantasizing about sawing my hand off. I'd been hoping the whole moon in all its dirty gibbous heft would come down and kill me. Do it. Getting this prescription for hydroxychloroquine (Plaquenil), by way of the eye exam, spelled the end of Prednisone, which had been the first and so far only solution to my suicidality.

But everyone looked so worried when they heard I was on it, like it was this angel you can only kiss so much, before it turns into poison or a person. Everyone made that certain face, when they heard about the Prednisone, like I was in love with someone in prison.

But now I was at the Moody Eye Clinic and it was only promulgating more problems! These narrow angles in each of my eyes!

I went upstairs and another ophthalmologist confirmed, after some hours, that I was in danger of sudden blindness, the shapes in my eye (the angles) told her so, just as the initial assistant had found. I should get a laser surgery, it was determined, which would effectively drill holes into each of my irises, preventing this sudden blindness from ever popping out its crazy claw and crossing out color, and more, *shapes*, for a forever, my forever.

We would have to schedule this surgery out, but in the meantime, I was to hurry down to the basement of the clinic and there a technician would collect photographs of the insides and especially the backs of both eyes, which this second-floor eye surgeon would need later, to calibrate her aim.

I'd been at Moody for over eight hours and I was starving, shivering. Going mad. The photos in the basement took hours. The technician kept swabbing my eyes with these long, dark Q-tips, and force-feeding my bedraggled eyes more kinds of drops, some cherry red, that she held above my face imploring my eyelids stay stretched by her assistant, widely, and that they be static for prolonged sequences while I waited for my corneas to once more feel the staining splash, and to keep my eyes open for more, new drops raining so slowly, a stuck rain that kept coming.

I left only when the moon was bright as a hexed white plate, so openly gibbous that night, the moon confessing it was whole, that it had been this whole time, and I was faint from lack of food and water, my body empty and cold and my eyes fortuitously weeping. My fingers, as ever at that time, now that Prednisone was really over, were frozen and painful, from the autoimmune disease that was the reason for all of this — the eye exam — in the first place. I cried walking home, my phone long dead, my nipples at this point in the cold practically bigger than my small, beautiful breasts. My nipples were so long and uninhibited by the decency of a padded bra and so they pointed at everyone, at children, pointing at the parked cars, they pointed to my apartment, at my boyfriend, Mari.

He was sitting in our little living area, with Janine.

I was so upset by all of this, and busy, too, with the other, realer-seeming diagnosis, my autoimmunity, and so tired from being diagnosed, and from all the panic, the practical suicidality, that pain releases. You think: I can't. So I didn't leap to go back to Moody.

But then I received a call only a few days out from yet another assistant — a medical student — from the second floor, where I had seen that more specialized surgeon, where I'd been ushered upward in a state of grave emergency by that doctor — that priest, that actor!

They were saving me, that was the tone. They, the whole group of them, had acted so very Hippocratically freaked out.

The medical student said, on the phone, that she was looking at my pictures, the ones that the basement technician took so far past the clinic's closing, and she — this student — had got so scared for me. She'd had to call.

"The way your eyes are shaped, with the narrowness of your angles, it could happen at any time. When you go from dark to light. You'll go into a dark movie theater for a matinee, spend two hours marinating there in that false darkness, you'll walk out into the true sunshine, and that will be the switch from dark to light that will end up blinding you immediately."

She really talked like this. Like out of a novel or from a script. It almost sounded like something I would have written.

"Please," she said, "this is so important."

She sounded scared. It sounded like we were in a movie. I was walking down Chestnut Street near the university — one of them — in the early afternoon. I told her I would think about it and then only a little later in the afternoon, massively worried, I called to make an appointment for the surgery. I asked for this same assistant, the student, so I could reassure her: I was good and would be taking care. But the receptionist on the phone told me the assistant had — *she wasn't going to be back.*

The woman on the phone sounded very raw, and as if she had already said too much, why else would you disclose any of this to a patient? I explained the conversation that I'd had with her, the woman who apparently had disappeared — honestly, it sounded as though she'd died or something, got hit by a car, a bus, getting lunch or something, it was really strange, had she died only minutes after I spoke with her? It really seemed like something vastly negative had happened to this person. The receptionist was trying to hold it together, actually. She made an appointment for me for two surgeries, six months out. First for one eye, on December 26. Then, I could do the other eye about a month after that.

"Will I be OK for these six months? I guess I should not see any matinees."

"What?"

About a year after the surgeries I saw a completely different ophthalmologist.

I'd had to switch insurance, my care turning bronzer by the minute, and he was associated with a different university's hospital. To go to him I walked deeply into South Philly via Broad Street, and the clinic was street-facing, the waiting room rectangular and normal, not a waiting arena with tickets like a butcher. His assistant had a wonderful technique for putting drops in the eye which has nothing to do with that *Clockwork Orange*-y way. He simply asked me to close my eyes. He placed drops on the corners of each eye. Then I could open my eyes and the drops slid right into them. It was so easy.

Why hasn't everyone been doing this drops method for all time, since the birth of saline? You have to wonder but humanness is such a process, even the most obvious things like a very simple way to administer eye drops or famously, knowing *not* to put leeches on people's skin, takes time and maybe instances of incidental insights, if that. Why did we even stop with the leeches? What was it? I doubt it was out of an observation about what bloodletting was doing! Maybe it was more, boredom, or a lack of leeches that season... But more, doesn't the for-profit essence of our medical system render the Hippocratic Oath its opposite?

My new ophthalmologist on Broad Street looked into my eyes — I mean in a technical way, with a machine — and said, "I'm so sorry you're going through all of this." He was referring to my fingers, half of them frozen lately into a crook. "I really hope the Plaquenil kicks in — or if not something else. They are developing new drugs for what you've got. You really have a reason to hope."

He said, "You know... Moody did you dirty. They did this surgery on you for no reason. You were in no way — I'm looking now — a candidate for this surgery."

I had wide, normal angles.

They put on a good show, didn't they. Put me right in their movie. But it's so much worse than that, because the second time I'd went, for my second eye, that second floor ophthalmologist pulled the goddamned trigger too hard. The laser had gone through my eye and *singed* the area directly behind it, in my brain.

In the novel I'd managed to publish right before all of this started up in 2016, titled *Naked Grapes*, I had written: "An eye is but a bubble blown off of the brain." But a bubble. Ha.

My eyes are not like bubbles, that was such lyrical drivel. I take it back. My eyes are hard and the surgeon at Moody had had to keep shooting the laser at me, acutely hammering her hole in with something that felt like a little pin, in size, but with a flat head. Each shot of the laser worked this flat-headed "pin" through me, finessing the hole.

It was not normal. The first time this surgeon did it, in December, it was not right, because I did not need the surgery — it was a scam — but it *was* normal. The second time, by February, she fucked up. The laser was too much. A *de trop* laser if I ever felt one — the pin flew and stung my brain.

And after that, I began having some cognitive problems. The best way to describe them is something between aphasia and writer's block. I could speak, and write, but I had become very spare somehow, unable to elaborate or more importantly to me, to use language — namely, *sentences* — elaborately, I mean with multiple clauses, which had always meant so much to me, to do that, to keep going.

I should say one more thing about this final ophthalmologist, on Broad Street, the last ophthalmologist I ever saw (because Plaquenil was not effective for me — I stopped taking it after about a year so stopped needing these worthless baseline eye exams).

This final ophthalmologist, he wished me well about my fingers. Other expressions of care have followed as I've learned more about my autoimmunity and whom to trust, whom to see, what to allow to happen to my body in times of distress and how to wait without a death wish, even in some pain or in, *pain* ... but he, an eye doctor, and over a year into the diagnosis, was the first from the medical profession to say anything like that, this expression of sympathy — familial, dare I say considering the topic of *Naked Grapes* (patricide), fatherly.

It made me jerkily weep, later, this ophthalmologist's care and concern, in front of Mari, as if my eyes were vomiting up all the eye drops they'd lately been forced to eat. There they all were, all the drops, regurgitated on tissues and between us, dropping on the table, which is when my boyfriend decided to say, as I was crying already...

He said he was sorry to be in love with Janine. He was sorry.

This is all a revelation. You can tell my speech — my writing — is not terse, so stuck and plain, what it was for years, and all through the early stages of the pandemic, after the laser. For a while I pursued this as a medical injustice. I sought, out of pocket, some MRI images, talked on the phone with my mother's friend, an entertainment lawyer, but I was tired, dealing with a new autoimmune disease that Plaquenil hadn't helped with, so on to other drugs, and moving out of my apartment — the breakup — so I didn't pursue anything, not really, but tea, masturbation, a very little amount of light reading, like, magazines. *Highlights*. I had a CD with 10,000 dollars in it. I started living in a walk-in closet for $600/month on Mole Street, in a southerly South Philly on what, to me, was the wrong, caféless side of Broad.

OK there was one café.

Ultimo.

I had been living before with Mari in a leafy, historic neighborhood up behind the museum, in a studio in the trees, that was like its own hoisted parquet-floored onion at the top of our landlord Janine's twin Victorian. So now you see why it was me doing the moving out! Moving from there to South Philly like this, it was like a vacuum comes for all the trees and you have nothing, you treeless fucking person. There aren't any in South Philly. Any.

Not on Mole.

In my closet room, Maron's clothes hung darkly just inches above my cot (lest you think she ceased to use this as a place to store them) while I listened to the machinations of a bipolar (I was pretty sure) polyamorous homeowner and her four or so cis male partners.

Was it polyamory or sex addiction? Or boredom, or addiction to conflict, a fitful eros, so death-drive driven, it — the polyamory — made things roll and slam around, so that I felt, in my closet, like a little coffin rider out at sea, the waves of this more modern lifestyle slamming against the death box within which I was attempting, so idiotically, *so*, to live. I wasn't doing good. I was grievously injured from the second Moody surgery. And I was a sad sad case, I missed Mari — though Janine made all the sense in the world.

She had seemed the protagonist, as a homeowner might, and a sympathetic one as well, she had not raised the rent on us in all of five years, there on Baring Street, back behind the museum whose steps were markedly famous through a movie — *Rocky* (1976) — but were more personally famous for me, those nights as a teen that I was sitting there, the famous way the lights all the way down the Parkway turn green together. It's 2 a.m. It's 3 a.m. Turned red. Turned together to Janine.

So this was back rent, that's all, the raised rent I couldn't help always suspecting was coming even though Janine was nice, and cool, and said she'd never raise it. She knew how hard it was, she said, to be a creative, how unfair it was, and how random it was, she said, that while I was a writer working at Sea & Poison, she was a tenured professor of French literature.

On the lease application I had written under work "writer/Sea & Poison employee." She had laughed, startled at the slash. My slash existence.

"If you're a writer, why would you need to work at Sea & Poison?"

"I mean, my book — *Naked Grapes* — didn't make me money."

"You're saying you've written a novel, you're an author, and you need to be working at Sea & Poison? What do you do there? Do you work at a *cash* register?" She said "cash" as though it were in quotations, as if cash doesn't exist. I guess I have to give her that.

Had I said *Naked Grapes* was a novel?

I'm being hard on her here and I apologize. Of course she could infer it's a novel, what did I write, a nonfiction about nude, about skinned fruits? Obviously, no.

Janine, she was basically my age but seemed a world order older. I could see the outline of a seamless bra smoothing and supporting her petite breasts, stamping with its satin down on her nipples, so that her dress (a design of zigzags in leather offset by silk) was uninterrupted by any uncouth natality being extrusive against the coldish spring. It was springtime. She was smooth and important, and her dark curly hair, not dissimilar from mine, was managed it seemed with some kind of excellent oil, maybe of the coconut, I don't know, but her hair was so shiny and coily, and worn up in the kind of enviable barrette, the seething teeth of tortoise shell, that I was shocked — inspired, really — by the level of couthness that is after all possible. I felt really ashamed but had always found it so difficult — I do now — to get myself very much together. Should I, I felt, apply oil to my hair now which can look nice in the summer especially but in the winter, at times, looks like meatgrinded vulture feathers?

And then I began to wonder and wonder, a bit stunned and mawkish on the sidewalk that spring, I admit it, what is oil?

And didn't Janine know that many people live a slash life? Didn't she know writers are slashed in a few or many more pieces? I could only read her confusion as a performance of her own rarified security, being that rarefied professor with tenure and everything, but I liked my job. Sea & Poison was a nice place to work, better than the Ritz. The seniors rose higher still, they left, then I read, it was one of the last jobs in the world without surveillance, so one might... You can't even do that if you're a librarian! I didn't even specialize in fish, or wine. The only thing I could not do, truly, on the job was write. No one typically will let you do writing.

They'll ask you what you're writing.

It was a shame. Working in fish, you have access to big sheets of paper — no lines either, which I prefer. And dark slavering pens.

Before my brain injury, I dreamed of writing on some of that fish butcher paper in ink on hand that almost *twinkled* it was *moist*, and it was burgundy that would take on a sunset coloration as it dried out, but my boss had told me: "That ink is expensive." It was, she said, a kind of heritage ink for fishmongers, allotted to the store a certain amount per year, and so I was overcome with respect and confusion and stayed back, in life.

"There's a Shusaku Endo novel," I told Janine out on the sidewalk, "called *The Sea and Poison*. But it's a coincidence. The owner doesn't know anything about that."

"Endo had an obsession — an interest — in the Marquis de Sade. He was very interested, in general, in France." Janine let me know.

"He was very interested in Catholicism, and Christ, and its viability in the East." I let her know.

We talked like this for a little while, having an Endo-off while Mari checked out the bathroom, Endo being best known for his novel, *Silence*, which was made into a Scorsese film. The toilet was a little bad. Its flush was a show flush, everything spun in an unswallowing circle, pieces of poop and TP on a merry-go-round, aimless like that. For fun. The ride, the centripetalism, only sullenly ceased and the different pieces of waste then hung about, the ride, the pretense of fun or flushing, just, done — like objects in space.

"*The Sea and Poison* isn't one of his great novels, like *Silence*, or *Foreign Studies*," Janine contributed to our Endo-off. "I recommend that one — *Foreign Studies*. A young Japanese student travels to Rouen, the little French town where Joan of Arc was burned at the stake, and where Flaubert lived with his mother and niece. She was (the niece) an ingrate, made a horrible mess of his papers when he died. It's a hard thing in my profession. Very hard. But it's alas, in this Endo novel, only very boring for a young Japanese student to be in Rouen, even though it's a bit of a miracle he was able to leave Japan at all after the war."

"*The Sea and Poison* is his very best work, Janine. I keep different copies of it at the counter, for customers to sign their receipts on top of, and reread it enough to realize this."

How blood was described in it, I fainted. I was at the counter eating dried kiwis. Blood is flowing out of a medical patient, red blood, that is described as becoming not darker red but redder, red blood that *reddens* as it quickens and comes from deeper. That made me pass out. How can a primary color *increase*? Maybe it was the translation by Michael Gallagher, or did Endo want to say that primary colors are only opening propositions? Or the red did not become redder, this is a figure, it must be a figure, the red so easily could have become more maroon, or darker, or deeper and thicker, but why did it become more of itself when it was not initially pale? I could not get over this. I could not understand this. A figure for what? I fainted at the impossibility of the sentiment and the sentence, as if it was the sentiment or the sentence, not the plot of the novel, that had crossed the Hippocratic Oath that is hovering by our skin, which these doctors, in that novel, routinely puncture. In Endo's *The Sea and Poison*, the doctors cross that hovering oath to open up so much skin in order to puncture their patient's lung, during World War II in Japan as it happened, to see how long being killed would take to make a patient — a POW — a dead kind of thing.

I fainted.

"I should imagine you fainted, Cumin. All that human vivisection, human evil. Mengele stuff, maybe it was even worse."

She looked at the lease application again. "Cumin Baleen."

I'm sorry about this. I guess I really hated her. And here I am painting myself the victim, poor little coffin rider. Of course there are trees in South Philadelphia. Just not on Mole Street. Not in my memory.

They are probably there.

I am looking it up just now, it's not quite how I remembered it:

> The Old Man and Dr. Shibata appeared at three o'clock, dressed in surgical gowns, their faces half-hidden by their masks. They were surrounded by the officers. The Old Man stopped for an instant at the threshold and glanced at Suguro
>
> — he is the young medical student conscripted to go through with it —
>
> who was still leaning against the wall on the verge of weeping.

What a victim! Everyone hates that. Everyone loves victimized people who don't act like it much, not seeing yourself that way, even if it's because you're a little idiotic. No one likes a crinkled little sour face in the corner going *you, you, you*.

No one likes a little closet-coffin rider. Maron, a "theater professional," was blatantly using me and I'd, I let her. I let myself be packed away in her closet. I let her let me know that I couldn't use my cell phone or laptop inside of it, lest the closet glower and wake her, past 8 p.m. I let her hang her long ravishing dresses in a line above my body, in pain.

Hydroxychloroquine, the Plaquenil, none of that had helped.

It was a low moment, a personal low. It was hard for me to triumph over Maron. So confident seeming, or I don't know, she was not neurotic. Not innocent but — guilt-free.

She had said, "If you want the spot I'll hold it for you for twenty-four hours."

She'd implied there were others waiting on this spot. A coveted spot. She was willing, she'd communicated, to hold it back and away from other people, so that it could be mine. I crumpled into her tactic, the most basic salesmanship, this mirage of demand. I didn't want to lose out on it. She said she got up at 6 a.m. and left the house for most of the day. That was something. I gave her a check for $1,800, first, last, and a deposit.

For the closet!

A little further into *The Sea and Poison*:

Then he quickly looked away and walked in. Behind him, with all the power of a surging avalanche, came the officers; but even they, when they caught sight of the prisoner lying face up on the operating table, hesitated for an instant.

"Go ahead, gentlemen. Move a little further up please."

Behind them Asai smiled just a trifle ironically. "As military gentlemen, you're surely used to the sight of bodies."

Janine called me, I was sleeping in my closet. Trying to. Maron was in her bed with someone new. They were rolling around going crazy. Sucking and grunting.

I believed she was living almost entirely on my $600, plus money she made renting her garage to a gig driver who slept in his car. She never spoke of another job or gig, a play or production, said she'd been out of work as a theater person yet she did leave in the mornings. Her house had two bedrooms, one of which she used in a very non-using way as an office, but she did keep a printer in there.

She might, she said, need to print something out!

She had handed me, actually, one morning a printed — typed-up — letter letting me know the rent, for the next month, would be raised to $650 to accommodate my use of a shelf in the bathroom, which she had not earlier, when I'd handed over my check, anticipated.

I was taken by surprise when I'd moved in, and carried my things past the unused office room, which housed only the printer, on its floor, and a life-sized stuffed leopard, something from a set. It lazed before the printer, like it was guarding its precious cartridge, the beating heart of any printer.

Why would this theater professional want a closet troll, not a real roommate?

"Hello."

"Hi Cumin."

"Hi … "

"I want you to know that Mari and I have ended things."

It had only been a month. A strong month. A sharp, a really good month, a precision vacuum that had eaten over a decade of me and him. We'd met at the Ritz, my first month working in the box office, I was 21. We went that summer backpacking around!

"He found a room in West Germantown, in this sort of split-up mansion."

It sounded charming!

The new person in Maron's polyrotation became surprised (being new) to hear a voice from the closet and he began to freak out, like it was a cuck situation, like my voice, in the closet, was the voice of an in-on-it cuck. He was saying things like "What the fuck" and "Who do you have in there?" and Maron was hastily explaining that I wasn't an in-on-it cuck but actually, her boarder.

"You have an empty room down the hall! I saw it."

The new person in the rotation was on to something, and it wasn't cuckoldry, he was beginning to understand. It was something more pathological and twisted but so normalized by privatization, by the rationalization of being an out-of-work artist, and by art itself. What an artist is owed. My landlord was, in her mind, a struggling artist. She had a leopard, too — her tattoo — on the skin in front of her heart. It lazily guarded that depraved cartridge!

This all felt very normal to Maron, the "theater professional," and she continued to calmly explain to the new man in her rotation that she used that space — the other room — as her office. The whole point of working hard enough to buy this house with government assistance for arts professionals was to finally have an office, she explained to him who sounded like he was getting dressed. I could hear the soft sounds of whipping, speeding cotton.

"But you have your clothes in there. I saw you get clothes from there. I saw you, when we came back earlier, throw your old clothes *into* there."

They had landed on my torso an hour earlier. "I don't have another place to put them!"

It was difficult for me to focus on both conversations, the soft and sort of solemn one I was having with Janine, the one I felt was a long time — well, a month — coming, and this one, out in the bedroom, which was loud and doing a lot to unscrew some of my screwiest victimhood. I knew it was not right how I was living, but it is so hard, in life, to get off of the nose. To climb out of your coffin. But people really need you to do that.

They get annoyed.

They get bored.

The new addition's voice, in combinations with the sound of him determinedly dressing, were making me want to burst from the closet. To run into his arms. To be carried by him out of that place. You and I, let's get out of here together!

A Philly meet cute.

"Janine," I said, "It's OK. I'm in a really good place right now."

"Are you sure, Cu, because I feel badly and I've been wondering if you wanted to move back into the studio — it could be for free, maybe for the next month? Whatever you need. I am truly sorry."

I burst from the closet.

I put my four paper grocery bags full of my things into Alix's car, a matte Volvo that said with a sticker that it was running on vegetable oil. I didn't understand how this was possible. I tried to remember what makes something oil, how an olive and vegetables and bones become oil. Is it compression? Is time a strong component? Why is something the oil of itself? Can people *be* oil or only very oily people?

In the car, Alix pressed me.

"Why were you living in that closet? It's not hard to get a room in Philadelphia, there's a lot of that sort of thing in West Philly. Are you into her?"

"Aren't you?"

"I feel gross I put it in. I didn't know she was such a pig."

"Well. She's beautiful."

She had big things, like, big points, a tight waist and large breasts, a height, a high heel, yet all passing through a glittering ditch of Daniel Day-Lewis–ishness, she resembled that marvelous retired actor. Like a goth deer. She took this kind of guilt-free care of herself. And her closet, I am on authority here, had been full of velvet and ravishing outfits, and these indexes of velveteen hems swayed on my face, and I exhaled sleepily, in sleep, into the bottoms of these dresses too porous to ever inflate fully with that oneiric exhaust of a woman closeted in a crossroads situation, now 37. Me.

"Maron *is* very beautiful. I've worked with her at Moody — the eye clinic? — for a year now, and tonight was the culmination of all our sexual tension. I thought it was gonna be so great."

He looked at me a little disappointed. I was such a different type than Maron. Now trying the next drug up from Plaquenil for my condition, a drug called Methotrexate, and losing with it a bit of hair.

Methotrexate

"YOU WORK AT MOODY?"

"I work there with Maron. I guess it's going to be awkward now."

"What floor?"

"Zéro." He said it in French. Blowing the *o* at me.

Was he in the picture-taking department, I wondered, and I told him I'd had pictures of my eyeballs snapped over a few tortuous hours down there, on the zéroth floor some time back.

Was he French?

I didn't feel any of this as interesting or a coincidence in that moment, though now it surely comes into focus as a big one. But that is because I am organizing a novel now best I can, amidst the rivers and the piles of everyone, and walking only a broken, only an overgrown and burnt road in my mind. It *was* a major coincidence, or consequential, even the brain-injured can start to realize that, and I feel it that way now, now as I'm writing it, I understand now that I am obviously reporting a *major* coincidence, that I am writing a novel, which is formally mostly an inventory of coincidences, but at the time you have to understand I was just another Philadelphian, someone who is quite used to meeting people who work at a university or a hospital in different combinatory amalgamations, it's common.

There isn't an array of industry in this chitchat city.

I recall, if anyone, Cecelia, the protagonist of Donald Barthelme's short story "A City of Churches," who discovers she has moved to a city of churches! Try that for a whole novel or a whole lifetime lived largely in Philadelphia. I was Cumin Baleen. I was raised in Germantown. A surgery scam had *singed* my brain. Everything was a hospital, a clinic, everyone worked at this, a kind of immunity against coincidence or the novel. Sea & Poison was hardly even an exception. We shared a wall with LabCorps, how else was I able to get my draw, give sixteen tubes of blood each tube redder than a vinegar pressed out of red lights on the Parkway all at once turning red, pass out for ten minutes, then return in time to relieve a junior who would soon become, in a swell, a senior at whatever, at I don't know probably the University of Pennsylvania.

Now, sure, now it's all coming together. Nothing ever more you hear here shall be deemed coincidental. What am I doing? I'm writing this novel. Here it is. What is oil? I must turn all the coincidences inside out like sweaters so as to view their massive networks. There are maps inside the sweaters.

More out of *The Sea and Poison*:

> After they did as he suggested, the officer with the underdeveloped moustache, still intent upon currying favor asked, "Hey, you, is it all right to take pictures during the operations?"
>
> "Of course, of course. We, too, are going to take some. Someone is coming from Second Surgery with an 8mm movie camera. The experiment is certainly an important one."

Alix told me he transferred to Moody from working as a nurse at yet another hospital, attached to a different university, one of the other many hospitals here. He told me about it while parked outside of the old studio, Janine's Victorian, where I'd directed him to drop me off.

We talked for a while.

"If a patient *toilets* well, did you know they have a seventy-five percent chance of not returning to the hospital in the next five years? It's the most important thing you can do for someone. And all we have in society is the bedpan, which is fucking uncomfortable, and most people can't relax and do it for the first days, which like I'm saying predicts their backslide. And death."

Alix continued.

"I became the go-to person. People relied on me probably too fucking much. Though I could only help males."

He pronounced "males" *mal-leis*.

"You don't do cross-gender toileting, Cumin. Ever."

He went on.

"I was asked to formalize my process, because all of the patients in my charge did very fucking well and recovered unless they were going to die anyway. Toileting is as important as a surgeon's skill — if you don't toilet your patients well all this good surgery is going to waste. I was asked to develop a workshop, because no one could figure out why I was so good."

Alix was probably an American. He sounded like someone who used to front a punk band in America but came later in life (he seemed early forties) to nursing, I think he thought nursing was good positioning for punk attitudes, the ways you liaise sometimes through the doctors — across, against — and the system, the way nurses have craft — *the materials* — on their side, and we talked for some time outside of Janine's — I note now I noted only vaguely then, I had not needed to give him directions to it — about fecal matters.

"I had never thought about it formally before, never considered my technique. But then I had to think about it. What is it I was doing, Cumin?"

He was like one of those talkers, I had to clock, who include you by name as a means to keep going, to talk more. Your name is like this petal they keep ripping and sniffing while they are talking, more. I was growing very restless, encountering this known technique. As long as he kept saying my name it could go on like this for a long while!

"What exactly am I doing when I do the bedpan, Cumin? Surgeons would be jockeying to get their patients into my area. I had doctors taking me out, bringing me to a Starbucks, giving me a Starbucks gift card for, like, a hundo. So, Cumin, what was it?"

He kept the car running, telling me.

"I was doing something specific to make them defecate, Cumin, and it *was* transferable, though — and this is sad — not for females. You couldn't use it on a female."

He pronounced "female" *fuh-mal-lei*.

A fuh-mal-lei ... A Starbucks ... His article usage made me again think he was actually French, or maybe something else.

"Were you giving out laxatives?"

"No! That's not what this is about! They all get a lot of laxatives anyway."

"What about an enema?"

"We don't have that kind of time! God. An enema is for, I don't even know, Obama."

I told Alix I really had to get out of the car now. I had to check in with Janine, to get the key to the studio once more, now that she really had broken up with Mari.

Janine and I became almost friends. I drifted downstairs at times.

She offered me that famous fuh-mal-lei agglutinant — tea, some peppermint tea.

We rarely talked about Mari.

"His work! He was gone all night. That can't work out between people in a real relationship."

Mari worked at that time as a private detective. It's not extremely dangerous, usually, but you have to work in the night. Mari approached couples at bars, or places like Steven Starr's group of restaurants, The Continental, Little Nonna's, acting as someone they might swing with (he tried to stay nice and slim), then came out of a bathroom back at someone's place or at a hotel with his phone. Taking pictures for family court, divorce, etcetera. He had a working person's gun.

"I was scared all of the time, for the whole month we lasted, Cu, about him getting murdered. A lot of people keep guns loaded in bedside tables."

"It's hard to be with him."

"He slept all day."

I told Janine over tea about what happened with the laser at Moody, how it had gone in too hard, and clipped me, bit or burnt me, *something*, in the brain. How after it happened I had stopped writing. And how when I tried to write again, like in a journal, low stakes on the metal stairs that led up to my studio — my own private entrance, very nice, and lately all for free — only very stuck, plain sentences came out.

"I am here."
"I see a dog."
"I can see the sky."
"I have a knee."
"My heart hurts."
"I will swallow a breakfast soon."
"I am here."
"I am here."
"I have a doctor's appointment."
"I am here."
"I love you."

Not necessarily nonsensical, not garbled in grammar or meaning, but also, nothing. I tried to keep making these statements, to keep my brain warm, or I don't know, to not forget how to write. I didn't know, those days, if I was getting worse or better or had I plateaued into writing with basically only baby building blocks, these soft polypropylene-like constructions like "I love you."

"Surgery scams," I said, "are so prevalent..."

Janine looked at me pointedly. She took a performative breath and said, "Cumin, have you ever considered that the ophthalmologist, at Moody, was trying to look out for you? What if his assistant really did see something that was off? The other ophthalmologist said they 'did you dirty,' but why do you believe him? Because his assistant had a better technique with eye drops?"

I couldn't believe it.

"All I'm saying, Cu, is how are you to know, really? What if they did save you from sudden blindness, or the possibility of getting cataracts later on? The surgery you got seems low impact, and kind of valuable, like something I might want to get considering what I've seen with some of my older family members."

I sat there.

"And who is to say if your brain got injured. Have you ever considered that what you have on your hands is some extreme writer's block? I wonder sometimes if you've got, like, a victim mentality. Think about it. Look at where you moved after the breakup. You know you didn't have to go live in that closet. Have you ever considered that you have a propensity to think that people are harming you? Or maybe to even put yourself in these sorts of situations?"

At that point, after another doctor's appointment — because nothing, not the Plaquenil, now not Methotrexate, was doing anything — I was trying a new drug for the autoimmune condition called Orencia. It was in need of refrigeration. It felt cool to inject, and as it was summer and Janine's central air didn't extend into the studio — but who complains when rent is free? — I enjoyed this brief reprieve of injectable air-conditioning, chartreuse and at great expense to the government, I guess, but why don't they regulate anything at all, but where there's regulation there's corruption, and this Orencia mercifully chilled the inner flesh above my right or left knee for a moment, for thousands of dollars, as I alternated each week the knee being offered to a needle, all alone in my free, hot studio on a mission to bend my fingers again and to think.

Orencia

I THOUGHT ABOUT ALL THE THINGS MARI MIGHT HAVE said to Janine within a single month. Things about how I get electrified by paranoia, and that I hold (it's the truth) a host of holy grudges. I started to wonder what she knew, what she thought of me. I began wondering if anything unpeppermintward was happening between us!

"Mari told me you were getting pretty paranoid. About Moody, he told me, but also other stuff."

I thought he must have said something to Janine about the desert. That must have been it.

We had gone to a sound bath in Joshua Tree, on a trip. I was turning thirty. After the bath, when everyone was really relaxed, and kind of banged on, a little banged open, we were speaking to a young man and rolling up our mats. He had walked to Joshua Tree barefoot from a different state, I don't remember where but from far away, someone who hadn't fit in with his family or his undergraduate institution, something... He had walked through his spring break into a hole into Joshua Tree. A good-looking person, with a fashionable, like a Spanish mullet.

"You love Adolf Hitler?"

Later, when Mari and I were in our young yurt, the young yurt in a development by Target, I said, "Can you believe that, saying that I said to him I love Hitler? What was that?"

Mari didn't know what I was saying.

"When we were talking to him, after the sound bath. All of

the sudden he asked me, 'You love Adolf Hitler?' like he'd heard me say 'I love Adolf Hitler.' Like *he* was shocked."

Mari had been standing right with us. We'd all been talking. But he didn't know what I was saying.

I knew I looked very Jewish. That is another thing, another trait. I know I look very Jewish. I'd been asked, for instance, by naïve fellow freshman at my own undergraduate institution in the Midwest (I dropped out before spring semester of my senior year) if I'd ever been in an accident, like, in a car crash. Because of my big bent nose. These were innocent questions, innocent enough, these young people from farming areas outside of that urban area now pursuing the arts to whatever degree had never seen a bent-nosed person who is — being Jewish is such a thing — *anything* in this world but an accident!

A Jew is not exactly a spontaneity.

I wasn't very religious but in this city of churches — the Midwest I mean — I became more Jewish it's true, in the way that one becomes a woman by way of her treatment, by way of the rut the certain repetition of treatments makes of one's initially puffed path. Someone uses a knife on puff, stabbing and rutting the life path, either quickly in one attack, or two, a quick swipe of the knife on puff, or there is a slow dragging of a knife for a long time, or quick little stabs at all hours, feels like shingles, or maybe it's little interruptions or exclusions, a realization that young boys don't look up to you or want to become you. A realization that Jewish women were forced into sex slavery at the camps, for use by guard and prisoner.

I knew that when I was young.

I think those freshman, when I, also, was a freshman, they were naïve. They'd grown up in high schools and towns and even cities where people looked more flat, more symmetrical. They did not expect a nose to naturally bend in such a warped, bony way. Probably, these Midwestern freshman were sheltered. Very sheltered.

It was only 2001, during some late August freshmen art school orientations, so the popular culture also was very sheltered. We had minutes more of that!

"Did you say you love Hitler?"

The young desert rat was saying heil Hitler to me! In a curious way. He was stuffing Hitler, that suicide, that arts school *reject*, in my mouth!

Mari said in the yurt he hadn't even heard that happen at all!

"Have you ever considered that Moody, maybe," Janine continued as we talked over tea, "is more cautious, a more conscientious place, than where you got that second opinion. That they see so many more patients and after all, are part of a superior hospital system? Think about it."

Moody was aligned, it was true, with the university Janine worked for, that had given her tenure at a young age — thirty-two — for her monograph on the famed Oulipian writer, Georges Perec — OuLiPo, that French writing group famed for writing with certain constraints.

That workshop for potential literature — Ouvroir de Littérature Potentielle.

Janine said she was sorry. Janine turned on Mazzy Star. Janine fed her gray cat, Marigold. Janine said she was pretty tired now.

But I wasn't hallucinating! Mari was maybe stoned or distracted, or deaf from listening to bells for an hour. It was the perfect time for that asshole to say Hitler to me, in a hippy, a healing environment. To *heil* Hitler. Or Mari started dissociating because it was crazy what was happening, but a Jew doesn't dissociate, I doubt it.

Mari was one of those Unitarian Waldorfians, who'd been encouraged.

We'd met in the Ritz box office, during that blockbuster opening weekend for *Brokeback Mountain* (2005). I'd been hired in a pinch, as people — lone cowboys, single men in wide, grieving hats, incredibly on-the-nose people — began camping along the cobblestones of the Old City neighborhood in order to see this film. It was hard for me to understand the box office system, and I became confused by the difference between receipts and tickets, which astonished me every time by coming from the same miniature little receipt-and-ticket printer.

Mari helped me out as we, together, helped Philadelphia see *Brokeback Mountain* over the course of a season, the entire theater was dedicated to it. It was a pure decade before the end of any ban on gay marriage. Imagine. No other films played at our Ritz for a long long time. Jake Gyllenhaal died on all screens eight times a day, of culture and masculinity, of murder that's reported as an accident. We watched a wounded people, from our box office tank, stumble into that sudden light (if it were a matinee) at that time so unaware of the 2015 decision, Obergefell v. Hodges, or of Heath Ledger's death in three years.

"Why did you drop out when you were so close to graduating? Aren't your parents pissed off at you?" Mari asked in our box.

"My parents?"

I drifted from Janine's kitchen into her living room. Her built-in shelving was filled with white Gallimards, yellow PUF editions, stacks of *French Vogue* and *Paris Match*, oeuvres of every Oulipian, plus everything ever published by two contemporary French writers, Marie Darrieussecq and Marie NDiaye, in precise and impudent alternation across a stretch of shelf and really it was so impudent, I mean, considering that NDiaye had accused Darrieussecq of *plagiarism* — and then, not of sentences, not in this sense at all, but of stealing a type of *plot* that NDiaye considered her hallmark, about sudden disappearance, and which Darrieussecq wrote of in her novel *Naissance des phantoms* — the narrator's husband disappears out of nowhere but doesn't a sudden loss belong to anyone, just suddenly so much?

I wondered how Janine felt about this particular literary debate, then laughed to realize that if my heart was with Darrieussecq, if I felt that you can't steal writing by its thoughts and plots, only by the way of its fallen sticks, its sticks and syntax, then I'm sure Janine felt the exact opposite.

I was sure in fact she felt for NDiaye!

We were like that, always opposed, from that Shusaku Endo—off on, I thought, and I laughed and snorted and picked up, with a kick, her own stupid monograph on Perec, with the intention of laughing at it, and scoffing at it, and reading the back for only more fodder to hate the woman who stole my boyfriend. It was facing out on her shelf, so proud, so monographic, good work, Janine, A+ (I guess we weren't really becoming friends . . .), and what was right behind it?

Naked Grapes

"JANINE LE MARIN DRAWS A LINE BETWEEN THE WORK of Georges Perec, a famous orphan of the Holocaust, and the diarist Anne Frank, and asks, Is there a bigger constraint — OuLiPo or otherwise — than genocide?

"Is Anne Frank *in fact* our signal Oulipian with her infamous limit on paper to write with, on lit writing hours? The constraint of her blithe older sister, Margot, the constraint of keeping constant company with the van Pels?

"Le Marin suggests that hiding from Nazis was the first Oulipian exercise *ever* (though OuLiPo as a practice of literary constraints officially begins in the '60s) and demonstrates Perec, one of the movement's famous members, to be a writer in the wake of Frank's astonishing diary."

A Jew does not become much astonished, I don't find. Was I *astonished* by the miniprinter in the Ritz box office? No.

But I've always felt disoriented and overwhelmed before a wage.

Perec who wrote an entire novel without using the letter *e*.

Why would you assume there could be an *e*? Why would *e* always be there?

An *e* like anything can be sudden, gone, suddenly taken and exterminated. Don't be so astonished.

You write without paper, sunshine or electricity, without your adulthood down the line, without any *e*.

How does Perec spell Anne Frank? That old joke ...

Ann with no "e," Ann of Amstardam ...

Imagine Perec in Paris, in the '60s, writing in his journal at a café, bent down at an angle, a huddled slanting, and imagine he carried the annex, the Franks' and van Pels', and Mieps', their attic in Amsterdam, at the slant of his writing back.

Constraint, constraint, of not sitting up straight.

What was *Naked Grapes* doing behind this absolute garbage of an academic monograph?

"If you're tired, I'll go up to the studio," I called back to Janine in the kitchen.

"Were you looking at books? Do you read French?"

"Janine, would you let me know, did Mari move in here, when you got together?"

"He moved down here, yes, basically."

Had *he* put my novel behind her book on the shelf? To laugh? To mix?

I texted Alix.

Alix parked on Baring Street and we walked to the Moody Eye Clinic. At night it was large and gloamish with traces of the fungal. We rode down in the murksome elevator.

There is something I haven't mentioned about Alix, it's my rustiness in my writing still, or it's the hardship anyway of writing a whole novel brain-injured or no. You forget important points. You forget these people are characters and that readers are sometimes interested in them like that, in their traits, like my brown curly hair, my cracked-up face, the hole in my iris, and the other iris, as well, or for instance my extreme bralessness. My striped dress.

I didn't mention this from the beginning of Alix's characterization. But it's so important and especially now and it's never too late. Just tell them. Tell them what is actually going on, Cumin. Well, we were in the basement of Moody, in the heart of the crime, crimes — two holes — against me.

He was good-looking.

"All I had to do was go in there with the fucking bedpan, Cumin. With cordless headphones, I say hello to the patient, HELLO, HI, but distracted like taking a call from my girlfriend. I help the man get on the bedpan. I put him into the position. I say it's fine, don't worry, please don't worry about that, you're fucking paranoid, bitch, I'm working at work what the fuck, I'm doing my job, where the fuck do you think I am, and the bedpan is filling up. It's delicious. Bitch, whore. It excites and opens a sphincter. I make sure a different nurse comes in before me and puts on *Seinfeld* on the TV, too. They think it's reruns but we have a DVD cued. It's like this combo, this nostalgia, you know, Cumin, everyone loving up on the '90s like that, all that '90s TV and feeling comfy in Jerry's apartment, and in a Manhattan like that, in general, where like a fucking postal employee can pay rent and then I roll in on my 'phone call.' It took a sec to get the combo but it started to work absolutely. Really really good. And I could perfect it from there. Like, the episode where Susan dies and nobody fucking cares, when she dies in the hospital and they are like, com'n let's go get some coffee, combined with 'bitch' and 'you're fucking paranoid' combined with my loving touch, my expertise in getting the man into his position with the bedpan. It comes together, Cumin. It really does. It really really does, you know? *Everyone* started using my script. We got a stack of these DVDs. That was the workshop, breaking down this script, the combos, the certain episodes in combination ... which is what I do here."

He beamed like he was telling me he wrote for a living, like that exists.

We were in a black box theater on two opposing actor's stools, in the basement of the Moody Eye Clinic at 2 a.m.

And I understand that's a little strange. Not terribly strange in the compendium of things, but a little. Why is there a theater in the basement of a clinic? What is happening? A novel is like that, about something *happening*, which feels off, or false, to focus on that considering. Bodies have been changed into clay by gunshots and poisons, a perilous gas, any way at all to make the body slump and pile about, to act like a lot of pre-pottery by cause of sudden extinguishing, yet in novels people *are* good-looking. They have curly hair, or big dicks, get and don't get their tenure, or whatever they want, love, drugs, and apartments.

Alix had big dick energy.

BDE.

For perhaps a few different reasons, I didn't react completely to the strangeness of being in a black box theater just then.

Perhaps largely because this wasn't the first black box theater I'd visited, in Philadelphia, in a basement of a discordant (to the arts) building!

There was a black box theater in the basement of an office building on Walnut Street, downtown. I remembered it.

The actor Jason Miller — Father Karras, the younger priest in *The Exorcist* — was writing and producing a one-man show in 2000 and as a teenager (a senior in high school) I helped out with the production.

I took the elevator up with him to WaWa on a break.

I would sweep the stage, I was interested in theater. He told me about his experience with going into exile after *The Exorcist*, people couldn't handle seeing him because of how scary it was, Regan's — Linda Blair's — head twisting all the way around, an infiltrated tween who'd once been wholesome now saying cunt this and cunt that, telling her doctor to "keep your fingers away from my goddamn cunt."

Jason Miller — Father Karras — bought me bananas at WaWa. The asphalt outside of it, at that time of night, deep as we were into the rehearsal process, nearly it was midnight, was a moon-butterous blackbread I remember.

I was at that time practicing monofruitarianism.

I remember feeling sorry for Jason. Who would come to his show? I thought about Father Karras saving Regan, by jumping out of the window and falling to his death, Satan (or anyway Pazuzu) secure inside of him.

COME INTO ME!

Now Jason Miller was at the bottom of *this* building. He had fallen into this basement, in Philadelphia, which was, at least to the *New York Times*, the basement of New York. To me it has always been a city of hospitals.

Every night, though, the theater filled up. His show was reviewed positively in the alternative weeklies and in the *Inquirer*, and someone saw Camille Paglia there. It was me. Maybe I'd only been inflected by the propaganda of indie cinema at that time about washed-up men who can't make art or write any longer, but a basement will have you, mal-leis. An exilic teenager, a monobananarian, would sweep for you.

Jason Miller was dead in 2001, when I would have started at the arts college. I'm seeing this now, looking it up. Miller died, it says, with Satan inside or outside of him, it doesn't say, in Scranton.

I mean to say I had a possibly extra slow reaction to being in yet another black box theater in a basement in this city. I felt strangely normal on this night.

I don't remember the content of Jason Miller's show. I remember we talked about Artaud, about throwing blood on one's audience at times, but I can't remember if I was telling him about it or if he was telling me.

"This is where my *scripts* are rehearsed, Cumin."

The BDE of Alix was getting to me. A coin purse of leopard neck muscles was opening in my underpants!

"Do you even know, Cumin, what we do down here? Myself and Maron."

I did care. I did.

"Alix. I'm so sorry. I have to interrupt this, it seems an important thing, what you and her do. It's an important revelation to my novel and also, my finding out what this scam is all about, why I got a needless surgery. You remind me, I have to tell you, of Roger from *Doug* (1991–1994), but dragged through the most glittering ditch of Jeff Goldblum. Do you ever get that?"

"I have gotten comments pretty much fucking like that. Maron thinks I look like a sleazy guy who runs a broken spa in the desert so, yeah."

"I've been taking a new medication for an autoimmune condition, lately. It's called Xeljanz. I feel slightly nauseous on it, but it's the first thing since Prednisone that is causing my fingers to bend back toward me, I mean my palms. I don't know how to put it, this new medication is making me feel very turned on. It's the removal of all this pain. It's like all of a sudden this big Jeep I'd been driven in so many miles into a forest of thorns, of pain, has backed up, has backward driven back out and now I'm sitting here feeling really restless almost like I want to drive back into the forest, but I want to fuck."

Xeljanz

"YOU'RE LUCKY YOU FOUND SOMETHING THAT WORKS for that. A lot of people don't find the right drug for fucking years."

"I do feel lucky, Alix, but I feel restless. I've been in such pain before this medication. Pain is, I don't know how to say it, it's been uncomfortable. I've fantasized that the moon would do it. Shoot me? But it's such a bluffer. It's nothing, it's just a fluffball. If you want to be killed, talk to men. Talk to the men you know personally."

"You want me to fucking kill you, Cumin?"

"No..."

"Cumin. What?"

"I've been practicing saying all of this to you since we met in Maron's bedroom, when you saved me from that closet. It's not coming out though. I get weighed down mostly by metaphors. I once was asked, when I was pretty young, to tell a rabbi (during the service!) how I felt about the Holocaust in front of a lot of people and I said it was like all the letters in all the books ever were dead! I had really said a wrong thing! I was *trying* to say the numbers associated with genocide are as enormous as letters in their mixtures inside of sentences, I mean, language being infinite ad infinitum, etcetera, and you could constantly rearrange them constantly shooting them, constantly killing everyone. That's what I meant. My family was really disappointed in me after that day. I think they were mad I'd made a metaphor out of any of this.

Now I'm talking about a big Jeep. All I'm trying to do is say Hi, fuck me. We're in a theater. OK. Fuck me on this stage. Right?"

"Cumin, I live with a boyfriend."

A boyfriend...

"OK."

"I'm sorry."

"It's fine. I didn't know that though. I forget everybody's polyamorous, so multitaskish. I don't think people are rearrangeable at all, I don't. If we were letters we could never make any words at all, we couldn't do that. We couldn't be fucking off constantly into different arrangements, new apartments, this isn't *Dark City* (1998), which is required of the alphabet — pure frenzy — and if people were letters everybody would be asleep, to avoid the work, the toil and elan, of language. Or are you even polyamorous, or were you just cheating on your bf?"

It was starting to dawn on me that it was interesting, a theater in the basement of a clinic, like, what is going on, is Brecht, is Shakespeare, is Wendy Wasserstein buried in the bottom of Pennsylvania Hospital?

"What kind of sick plays do you write down here, you asshole?"

"'You're fucking paranoid.'"

"Something is wrong down here. Do you know about the scams they run here?"

I thought suddenly of *The Sea and Poison*:

"Are you going to cut here?"
"No, no lobotomy. Tomorrow Doctor Kando and Doctor Arajima are going to perform that sort of experiment on another prisoner."

"There are things so much worse than Moody, than Le Marin. She's honestly fucking nothing."

"Janine?"

"You know what they did at my old hospital? They raped women on the OB/GYN table. There's four of them. Four OBs who do it. They like them pregnant. They tell them to come in before they're due, I'm talking right before. Two days before. They put a sheet over the pregnant belly. Then they fuck her, saying they are using that wand. It's them. It's the skin of their dicks and their dicks inside the dick skin. Everybody knows. All of us nurses. I wasn't even on that floor. Everyone knows.

"There are policies. She can't have anyone in the room with her. No husband, partner, not even the sister comes with her. She can ask for a chaperone but that's what they say, a fucking *chaperone*. It's infantilizing. No one asks to be fucking chaperoned. These women are pregnant, maybe they don't feel very fucking assaultable in that moment, but that's when the OBs do it. There's four. Everyone knows which four. One of them is a 1% owner of the whole hospital. Two of them own 4%. One of them has been banned from three other hospitals. One of them is Jewish. You're Jewish. I could tell, the way your nose bone looks like the bludgeoned corner of a wire hanger. It's obvious.

"You'd think Jewish men would have some sense of history, but doctors across history have parted ways with Hippocrates, Cumin, who knows maybe Hippocrates wasn't always in line with himself, maybe Hippocrates himself was polyselferous and some doctors have, Cumin, if you want to get actual with me, done a human fucking vivisection."

A human vivisection . . .

"All things on the table at all times. If you're ever on a table for inspection or an operation, Cumin, I'd remind yourself that a doctor's table is upholstered in chameleon's skin. The disinfecting liquid they apply to it before each ride blanches its true nature, which is fucking *changeable*."

This was just awful.

"These women would give birth days later. It was perfect, Cumin. Because who has the energy when they have a new baby to try to say this to a hospital or hospital cops or the police or city.

Maybe they dissociated while it was happening. Some would *come back* to the same OB for the second time, having another kid. I don't know why. That's what's happening at my old hospital, so I work here, Cumin. There's no other job for me in this city of fucking hospitals. What do you think I'm gonna do after nursing school, go work at a car rental counter at the fucking airport? It's less bad what I do here. And Maron, she's no different than any other out-of-work theater professional. They all come work for the hospitals, acting as the patients and such, to train the fucking med students. Maron's no different if she happens to pretend to be a student herself, it's still acting, it's still a job, if she calls up our subjects like she's some fucking medical student — some *intern*. I don't know, Cumin. You know. What. Le Marin isn't so bad. She's minor. Just another humanist cobbling out an inroad to some of that sweet STEM cash, just another professor with a lab going nowhere, don't even mind her, Cu. She's insane. She sucks to work for. She has me writing up all kinds of scenarios and I'm good for it. She's paranoid we'll need all of these crazy conversations down the line. I go home to my boyfriend, Cumin. He doesn't know about the thing with Maron. We're not all polyamorers. I'm old school as fucking hell, Cu. What. What. Stop it. Stop. Hell yes she ordered your brain injury, but you'll be better for it, we all know it — a better fucking writer."

I am confirming it. George Tyndall, at USC, raped, assaulted, abused women in his office for over thirty years. Someone had said, "Unfortunately the medical assistants have worked with this for so long and feel our management has known about it, yet nothing has been done. At this point they do not keep track of specific names as it occurs every day."

Mahendra Amin, a sterilizer of immigrant women at an ICE facility in Georgia, performed vaginal ultrasounds by hand, "the most," said someone, "medical way of being raped you could possibly experience." I look up Nassar of Michigan, I look up Robert Hadden, his 245 victims, at least, from at least 1987 until 2012, his sexual assault of pregnant patients in New York City.

"Hello?"

Alix let me see a script he'd written for Moody. I imagined the sunrise outside was making the Cira Centre violetate. And I could hear the elevator moving in the building.

MEDICAL STUDENT

Oh, uh, is this xxxxx.

PATIENT [probable responses]

Yes.

MED. STUD.

I'm calling because you were here yesterday? I'm sorry, I'm flustered.

PATIENT

I was there yesterday. What?

MED. STUD.

You didn't meet me. I'm a medical student — an intern, I'm looking over the doctor's notes and the imaging you did for her, in the basement?

PATIENT

OK. Yes?

MED. STUD.

I'm sorry. Is this a good time? Uh.

PATIENT

It's fine. What is it?

MED. STUD.

I'm wondering if you were going to call to schedule out these surgeries.

PATIENT

Were you there yesterday?

MED. STUD.

I'm Dr. XXXX's intern. I'm looking over the images now. I haven't seen angles this narrow in any textbook...

PATIENT

OK.

MED. STUD.

It could happen at any time. When you go from dark to light. You'll go into a dark movie theater for a matinee, spend two hours marinating there in that false darkness, you'll walk out into the true sunshine, and that will be the switch from dark to light that will end up blinding you immediately.

PATIENT

I don't have cataracts in my family.

MED. STUD.

These are really narrow though. Your angles. It scared me so I called you. I'm not supposed to, but I don't want you to — promise you won't go to any matinee until you think about this.

PATIENT

I'll get a second opinion.

MED. STUD.

Have you considered that Moody, maybe, is more cautious,

a more conscientious place, than where you'll get that second opinion. We see so many more patients and after all, are part of a superior hospital system ... Think about it.

I flipped back through the script, since we'd started in the middle.

    OPHTHALMOLOGIST'S ASSISTANT
I've always suspected *I* was Nigerian.

I dropped out of arts college. Bas was in his late forties. We went to Europe together, his treat. Now that there are words for things there weren't, I've learnt this is called "financial domination." We went to multiple biennales. We went to Prague and London and Venice. At that time a few years after 9/11 a lot of new art was *transgenic*.

Goldfish turned to blackfish. We saw a clear carrot full of white hair.

Bas paid 2500 euros to drink its clear juice. He offered me a sip (it seemed to be water) and said, "That's 500 euros, for a sip. What will you do?" as if sipping the art he'd purchased to drink up had transgenicized *me* into a life of prostitution.

It was everywhere at that time, I'm trying to say — transgenic art.

Bas was a Dutch person living in the Midwest, not a professor, nothing obscene. A man at a café, the one where I worked, doing a little drawing. Sketching me. Someone with free time. We went to the Anne Frank House in Amsterdam. Some children pointed, saying I was her ghost, the uncanny resemblance coming to a head in that ground zero of resembling Anne Frank, as I always have, though I was becoming less a doppelgänger every day by the incident, each minute and day, of growing older than her.

There are several of us out there, as I have been told constantly all my life that people I meet knew or know someone who looks (or even acts) exactly like me — I have scared and disrupted people. And I have met people, face to face, who are almost me. Chocking it up mostly to overpopulation, an overwrought genome, but also sometimes wondering — paranoid — if I belong to an experiment, after all I do.

I put my face down in Anne's annex, bashful about freaking out anyone. A guard came up to say, "Wow." He wanted me to pose for a photo in her writing area, so slanted by cause of being an attic that I thought, had to, What does it mean to write under the sign of The Arrow?

The Sea and Poison:

> "Then with you it's just the lung?"
>
> "Yes, sir. I know there's no need to explain anything to you as a medical officer, but for the guidance of you other gentlemen, who are so kind as to take part today, I'll explain briefly what we are going to do. The experiment to be carried out on today's prisoner is a simple one. It is a matter of investigating to what degree it is possible to cut away the lung in tuberculosis surgery. That is to say, the problem of how far one may cut a man's lung without killing him is one of long duration in the treatment of tuberculosis and also has a bearing upon the practice of medicine in wartime. And so today, therefore, we intend to cut away completely one of this prisoner's lungs and the upper section of the other. That is, to put it into a nutshell..."

Bas wanted me, that actual night, to watch a film, *The Night Porter* (1974). Do you know it? He turned *The Night Porter* on at the central, lavish hotel in Amsterdam, where his father used to, he said, play billiards in big competitions, having brought the DVD (from the US!) in his bag. This is a film about a starving sex-starved woman and her Nazi guard, an infamous piece of Nazi kitsch. Bas wanted to watch it and touch me, which is to say there are histories of people, of guards, there are artists, bored artists after 9/11 certainly after 2001 after that first draft of the human genome sequence was released, who would be tweaking the genetics of another forgetful fish. There is experimentation. There are gaseous shower areas, a way to trip in Europe, and those trips to Europe in those early 2000s full of their own little problems.

There is — I'm trying to say — this great sense of experimentation in all of history, this need to experiment on the human, to puncture the human lung and *see what happens*, of human vivisection, to dig into eyeballs, and here I was so many years after the Holocaust and here was *The Night Porter*, and my groping older lover trying to experiment with a combination of that film and touching me.

I left that hotel (that night) in an überless Europa of 2004 in the middle of the night of that European ultra-Christmas before spring semester of my senior year. I camped out at Schiphol (pretty nice campground) for two days waiting to use my ticket home, dreading running into Bas but, I never saw him!

I assumed Bas extended his trip, being rich and possibly — is it possible? — embarrassed.

I'm trying to tell you: I wish I could say I was more surprised by this revelation in the basement of the Moody Eye Clinic, that it even *appeared* to me as a revelation, but I suppose I'd been primed, or the word these days is "groomed," to know all my life that experimentation, pernicious curiosity, is to be *expected*, so much so that when Alix said "It's not an accident, Cumin, at all with the fucking laser. That's Janine's," I only thought about Bas in Amsterdam squeezing my breasts as Dirk Bogarde, an SS guard who's only *posing* as a doctor in the film, takes pictures of Charlotte Rampling at the camp — at Schiphol I glamped hard and I started writing *the eyes are but bubbles blown off the brain* in my journal.

I've been experimented on. I'd, I'm saying, dated. But nevertheless I did ask Alix to drive me with my things (medicine, clothing) straight back to Maron's.

Daniel Day-Lewis. A deer. A female deer.
Danielle Doe-Lois.

"Cumin?"

"Sorry. I'm back."

"For how long?"

"I'm going to stay until I've used my last month's rent — and security deposit."

"The closet needs a repaint. You've scuffed it up."

"I'd like to stay in the office."

"I need to — "

"You lied to me."

"There's nothing I can even imagine you're talking about. God."

"You told me you were a medical student on the phone."

She sighed. She looked at me like, *this bitch*. Like, *God is EVERY day for this bitch?*

I kept living there, past the deposit.

In my thirty-eighth year I was going weekly for infusions of fish oil at a clinic in West Philly trying to heal my brain injury. I had stopped Xeljanz (alarming studies — death) and been put instead on Rinvoq, which allowed me, without incident, to live almost entirely how I had been before the autoimmune problem. My Obamacare rheumatologist didn't think it was such a big deal. He wasn't the type to think the moon should or even *could* be commissioned to hurt a suicide craver on a walk. He moved me forward through drugs until I felt a click. He hasn't been part of this novel, but in every novel many functional things, even in the medical system, might be lurking around. When I told him all about what I was writing, I mean before Moody and my brain injury, before I couldn't write, he told me to look at Helen Dickens.

Rinvoq

"WHO?"

What is oil, is it compression, is it essentialism?

This is unnecessary, but Bas died. I never, it turns out, had to be concerned about running into him at the café or around, but I had no idea he died until I moved that spring back to Philly and started working at the Ritz. If I had known, I might have graduated but I didn't like school, but I didn't know it — he died — until I'd gone out with Mari after the last *Brokeback Mountain* for the night, and we'd solemnly said goodbye to a lone and drifting last cowboy of Old City, and, in a fit of deviation, we chose a fine bar.

We usually drank until close at a shittier one, the last dive in Old City.

The fine bar was part of an international restaurant group owned by a competitor of the hotelier in Amsterdam, who had hosted those international billiards competitions in its grand lobby. The owner of the international restaurant group was a provocateur, an ex-partner of the hotelier, so suddenly Mari and I, in our black slacks and white button down shirts, magnetic name tags and New Balances befitting a cinema's staff were contemplating a craft cocktail menu that was in pernicious and mocking tribute to seven victims of the old Amsterdam hotel's gas leak, on the night — before Christmas — I'd fled, the porter of that fine old Dutch hotel still befitting of porters calling for me a black car (he told me he'd charge it right up to the room, no problem).

The cocktail menu in Philadelphia was "In Memorium" and

detailed the events of that evening in the tone of an old ghost tale —

The leak killed seven bachelors. As these were bachelors, lone men traveling to the region as is custom for its reasons, no one knew they were knocked out by the gas — no one found them until a cleaning was overdue. Nothing exploded. The gas blew in, killed them, then seemed to dissipate, so for a long time — until autopsy time — no one knew what happened at all. Were these bachelors in a cult, or a group secretly traveling together, was this organized or does life sometimes organize who dies, almost as a bowerbird will organize trash it finds by color, why were seven bachelors lined up alone in their beds and dead there? I was never listed as an occupant, a companion, a girlfriend, a person, I'm looking it up just now — I hadn't been there. If the porter from that evening remembered me at all, recalling the black car he'd ordered, he must have only thought I was a prostitute of the area, if one that looked a lot like Frank, but one hopes not as gig or gimmick.

"We mourn the loss of the seven old bachelors of The Klootwijk!"

#6. The Bas van Asch — absinthe, Sazerac, orange peel, and gas. Lavender oil.

Mari and I ordered two, eager to get drunk. The drinks were so strong, and big, we finally got together, peeling off black slacks and white button-downs back at Mari's rented room in his Gayborhood trinity, back in 2005 when a Ritz employee could pull off such a stunt, a room, at $6.25/hr.

The matinees at the Ritz were very popular with retirees living in well-appointed buildings around the theater. Some died at the Ritz. That happens. A good way to go, I've imagined. You put a velvet rope across the door. And the retirees with Parkinson's would be signing their credit card receipts so nicely. Their signatures were remarkable, the way old people have that over everyone, their penmanship, and you would never know the shaking group of flesh and joint, swerving and hopping up and down on top of the receipt paper, notoriously toxic to workers, could produce it.

Yet slowness and determination hisses a poison — a sedative — into shaking.

After my infusion of fish oil one day, in that thirty-eighth year, I took a train to Germantown. I was really stinking. People on the train moved, except one man who said I smelled good. He said he loved fish and loved to suck on their eyes like a candy. I must admit, I have enjoyed the same activity, and some of the mongers at Sea & Poison had bidden me to do the same and I liked it, but I couldn't bond with this man about our similar experiences and proclivities because he wasn't getting to know me. I wasn't there. When I got off the train he followed me, was behind me and in a way, he was out in front of me, dragging his knife slowly into the puff of my life path, but I walked on the bricky lane in the dark, those infamous (to me) bricks of Germantown like a patchwork quilt of red teeth you'd want to floss if you thought the worst of moss, but I do not.

Mari wouldn't close the door to his room in the mansion.

"Why?"

"It's the cats. They start to scratch and piss with fury if anyone in here closes their door, so we all keep them open. It keeps everyone very close, actually."

I hadn't seen any cats. "You've made friends?"

"We're a bit more than friends, I'd say now. The mansion's been turning into a bit of a ship. We're the crew, you know?"

He sounded strange, a bit of a Brit.

It had been a vocal arts academy, on Lehman Lane. The old teacher had lost his students. He was too old to teach, asking students for help with his care, including toileting, during vocal sessions. So they left, pursuing careers in opera and teaching. Now he had become this landlord for singles, gig workers, adjuncts, freelance detectives, but the cats had kept everyone's door open, even the bathroom doors had to be open, because the cats got really upset otherwise, and they would piss vengefully at the sound of one clicking door, would slit their own cat throats being incredibly cutthroat at the sight of a single lock, and nobody here, Mari said, had a problem helping the old vocal instructor with the toilet anyway. Quite the opposite. Nobody worked anywhere else anymore.

"At first we were coming and going, but you can imagine what that was like for the cats — the front door."

"Now no one works? No one leaves?"

"We don't pay rent, Cu. It's not like that any longer. We're a family, it's a bit of a ship. That all out there? It's water to us."

"Hard to pretend to *glide* through something as stiff as G-town, I bet, bricks and cobblestones and trees, all this history here — the forts, Mari, the forts — hard to make it all into water, don't you think?"

Mari told me he hadn't left the mansion in many months, not even to take a walk. He showed me the fineness of the bottoms of his feet, this sort of dusky whiteness like the salt flats of Neptune's notoriously dusky perineum, and his door was so knobless, so openly open.

Obligatory?

I wondered if Mari were suddenly in a cult or something, and I wondered if in the American medical system, in the nursing and in the American aging system, this is what's actually required to get any help with the toilet. Start a cult.

Mari's room was outlined on the inside with Borax, a white rectangle of powder that traced the room, to keep roaches presumably away from his mattress. That's what Borax is for. The ceilings were tall and you could see they'd been welted all over from operatic practice in the before times of this old vocal academy, or I could see anyway such vocal welts with my feelings which sometimes turn by swiveling in a shiver machine into visions, but I had no feelings for Mari any longer. That much was pretty clear.

It was actually over!

Maybe, too, in the American boyfriend system you need to see someone decimated and silly in a cult to get over them, I'm not sure. I'm not sure what it takes.

"I came over here to ask you, Mari, were you really ever with Janine? Were you even together? Did you ever even move in with her? I always thought our breakup was so odd. I mean, was it you, who put my book behind her stupid, stupid monograph on Perec? Maybe when you were living with her?"

"Your book?"

"*Naked Grapes*."

"I don't remember."

"Which part?"

"It's not interesting to me. It's almost time for dinner and I have to make two sides. And they *both* have to be green."

What did I expect, going there?

"Janine said your relationship ended soon after we broke up. I mean, what a waste, right?"

"The cats *all* had to go to the basement. To keep them safe from overboard. We've had to lock them away, but someone always brings them sides. They had to go down there. Litter boxes are dangerous on a wet deck in the hallways, sliding in a storm and could break someone's ankle. Now they're in the basement and are weaving, together, a brocaded floor of shit and this actually keeps us floating — did you know that cat shit is hollow?"

"Oh."

"Janine disliked *Naked Grapes*. She called it 'lyrical drivel' and she was gonna change your writing with her laser, do you know, Cu, for her monograph on Medical OuLiPo?"

"Medical OuLiPo?"

"Yeah."

"What?"

"How's it going? Are you writing shorter sentences at all? I guess she was gonna take a shot at that veritable wasp's nest of commas — clauses — in your head."

"Mari. I need those."

"Don't you wanna do more with your writing, with your life? Like not publish something yourself and hand it out to a few friends?"

"It was published by a small independent press that shut down, but whatever."

"Janine says you could be the next Shusaku Endo!"

"Shusaku Endo?"

"She said I *had* to break up with you. If you do Medical OuLiPo on someone and there's no other rupture, she said it's a real waste. The constraint won't stick much, she said."

"But Mari, I had all this new autoimmunity. Remember? None of my fingers would bend and I was hurting . . ."

"When you wrote your next novel, when you finally became successful at all this writing stuff, I was gonna call you. I was gonna tell you then. I mean, are you writing yet?"

Marius wet his little pinky and put it in some Borax on the floor and dabbed it on his gums — "This keeps my appetite nice and low."

"There's no roaches?"

"No."

Fresh Prince

MUSHROOMS WERE GROWING, IN MY THIRTY-NINTH year, in the burnt area behind my eye. I tried to think about it.

Mushrooms grow on burnt pieces of the forest floor.

OK.

What is different about "brain" and "forest"?

I don't know anything.

I am not aware of anything about the brain or oil. How is there oil? Where? Do you have to pressure the olive, or put undue pressure on an avocado — is there oil inside of mango? Is oil anything you press or pressure, can a pressure cooker make oil? Can you put a hand in a pressure cooker? Can you pressure me into an oil? Can the brain be squeezed? Or used very much by me?

I don't know.

I didn't *know* if a brain, in the way of a forest or a toenail, can grow its own mushrooms? Is it *itself*? Is it in the skull, but with the one road out, is that the neck? Can't you mess with someone's head, though, through their gut or, I don't know, by raping them? Aren't brain cells in the gut? I thought I'd read this...

Can mushrooms grow in your head if it is burnt? Are brains and bodies interchangeable, is a question, it's *my* question, but are brains and forests on a spectrum?

Can a forest have a reflex if you bang a hammer on a wild turkey in it? Can it try in its trees to learn French late in life?

Je ne sais...

I was tripping, that's what it seemed. I was tripping without ingesting mushrooms from the outside.

People's dogs had extra geometries, even saliva spilling on my hand when I greeted dogs (or when they came sniffing up to me at the café — I was there on Saturdays) had that nature of hard rhinestones studding my knuckles in a summer so hot, so mangoleaginous I sometimes thought I was peeing. But it was my sweat. It was my Swarovski body being pressed and popped out of my porous (I think? Are we?) skin as I walked around South Philly (treeless...) in my same striped dress without anything at this time underneath it.

A loose relationship with even your underpants signals, to me, a momentous time.

Your underpants in a momentous time have something of their own instinctive life, not always clinging about. Your underpants become sentient and independent some summers. And my heart, I don't know how else to say, it was a water bottle of fizzy booze lying in meadows of stinging sinew in the black air packed like black eels like sardines in a dawning tin?

I was still crushing on Alix. And lately I'd been taking my underwear off about it.

Is it OK to be this horny?

I was walking around thinking of Alix all of the time and his BDE. I was almost squeezing, holding, kissing, and loving anything I touched, the couch, certainly Maron's old theater leopard in my new pseudoroom with my printer roommate, though it smelled bad. Even the printer got my loving touch, and I looked at cracks in the sidewalk and street and thought about jamming my actual clit into them like a fin searching to surface in the inverse, getting off — I hoped it would — on the jagged way a crack acts. I wanted a crack in a sidewalk, basically, to use its crackling edges to stimulate me. I'm trying to say that I was looking with lust and erotic admiration at the sidewalk and at anything.

I thought about Alix and how much I wanted his cock inside of me including my blood cells and immune system which had been suppressed by the drug Rinvoq into keen submission and was ready for his domination but in fact he'd never called me after the night in the basement.

I'd texted ...

In the middle of the night I was going crazy, rolling around in bed and making myself come on a wearing loop. I had few means of expression! I thought about writing, and about that maxim about writing, about you need to fire a gun in the third act, and I thought COME ON. If this is a novel and there's a character introduced who has a hotness condition of BDE, doesn't his big dick have to be exposed and explode, down the line? Don't I get it?

I texted Alix a lot — my short, stalled sentences.

"I like you."

"Do you want to take a walk?"

"Can we talk."

I had the dog saliva of summer all over my fingers and I made myself come over and over with them, as they bent and sprang with ease, like a true Pavlovian who's made to come every time I think of that certain person with his big bell energy. Shit. Shit. That's all ... It was a predicament. Underwear get out.

I killed a succulent on accident.

But he was back with Maron.

"You think you're so crippled, such a woeful little crip," Maron said in our kitchen, two years into this more equitable living situation — I lived in the printer's room for free, on pain of what she'd been involved with. She felt bad, at least formally. "But if you tried to write now, you know? It would be better."

"You go on — you extend the sentence — because you feel bad." This was Alix.

I saw him on Saturdays at our house, before getting out of there. I always went to Ultimo for almost all of Saturday, because they rolled around sucking and fucking for such a long, long time starting in the morning.

"Brevity is confidence," he said.

Maron was as beautiful as Daniel Day-Lewis in his absolute prime, in *The Unbearable Lightness of Being* (1988). He partners with Juliette Binoche but cannot give up on "Sabina," the actress Lena Olin, a woman so intoxicating and sexual, as Prague erodes from was it communism? Binoche, his country waitress...

He is the philanderer, prepolyamorous. He famously says to quite a few people around the crumbling, tonally dark city, "Take off your clothes." Philadelphia, this city of hospitals and universities, looks like Prague a little if you squint and aim the sunset at certain bricks. And I suffered like a country waitress — waiting for Alix to just get over Maron/Lena Olin, but they worked together. She had whole days with him in that basement.

"Live here for free, I don't actually care," said Maron. She said, "Cumin, I'm sorry." She said, "But you know what? We need your sample."

Naked Grapes being the hideous control. Lyrical. Drivel.

Sea & Poison fired me. One of the last places to work in this city without surveillance or responsibilities, but they began to change. They hated what I wore.

My nipples were pointing out the dried fruits in plastic containers, the red snapper stuffed with saffron and dill, the wine. I was not looking sanitary or polite and I was stealing alcohol a little, I was drinking at work. Things were becoming corporate at Sea & Poison, not as if this little upscale market was some kind of commune before, or a Prague, but it wasn't so corporate but they were filming me now, being bought by a big hospital now, I'm sure, and because of how I was, how I dressed, it was almost the problem of me tricking them into making porn by simply surveilling me constantly. They had so much surveillance of my reading Endo, my nipples as apparent as truncated tusks under fast fashion cotton, and there I was evidently day drinking. They filmed, like a porn movie, my entire body including pussy and asshole lit up without any underwear on and my legs a little Balthusian I admit it with that porn style corner market lighting, but this was an upscale place. None of the chips for sale were very common.

Alix was really back with her. In her polyamorous universe he was "Saturday." I think that's a compliment. He came over one morning with a bag of new sex toys. She liked that stuff a lot.

Maron showered, preparing for their sex, and we sat in the kitchen with the bag from Condom Kingdom on South Street between us on the table.

"But you *are* cheating?"

"Not anymore. I told my bf because honestly, Cu, we're serious..."

No wonder, I thought, Mari had to join that cult. There's no work for anybody, nothing good, look at what happened to me at Sea & Poison, they got uptight, and certainly there's nothing anymore for a private detective specializing in catching cheaters considering how filthy the word "monogamy" is, how gauche it would be to cheat or care.

Alix said, "These days it's on the fucking kitchen calendar that I come here."

"Let me see."

He'd brought a toy that spoke up as a dick Teddy Ruxpin. It was more than I could bear. It was a big brown dick in a vest saying all of the old phrases!

"Can you and I be friends?"

"There's nothing in the world like a good friend."

"I really enjoy talking to people."

He'd bought a vibrating madeleine butt plug.

Proustian sex technology, that madeleine more retro of a sex toy than a dildo of Ruxpin, who I myself remembered fucking as a child, turned on by the hard area of his tape deck in his stomach, the sudden plane of hardness so vibratory with such speeches, storytime, offers of friendship. I mounted that hard area of the tape deck on Ruxpin's tum like a dolphin hopping on a dais at a questionable spectacle, but nobody questioned SeaWorld then.

"A madeleine butt plug, wow, was this Maron's request? I didn't know she read literature. Is she interested in the totalizing *evacuation* of anything that is at all quotidian, to be replaced not even by a sense of a *present*, or the past, but rather the extreme formation of an *instant* around which a song of possibilities twists, is that so? Honestly, I've never seen her reading much French literature, what is this, for Janine? Are you honestly fucking both of them? Wow."

I held on to the butt plug, to its formidable base.

"Cumin, you're fucking tripping. You think Condom Kingdom sells madeleine cookie butt plugs à la Proust? You think Condom Kingdom is interested in the experience of magical fucking simultaneity as expressed by Maurice Blanchot, which you seem to have no problem plagiarizing in casual conversation? That's fucked. You think I'm fucking Maron and Janine? Maybe, but Cumin, get a grip this is a fucking Glade PlugIn with Shell Design. And you know why? Because it's getting a little rank upstairs."

He looked at me like I was rank.

"OK I didn't see there was a separate CVS bag in here. Sorry."

"It's fine."

"I didn't know they still *made* Glade PlugIns."

"Sorry, Cumin, but honestly listen. If Janine doesn't see a sample, she's gonna fire us. I don't know if Medical OuLiPo takes a lot of time or what but it *should* work. It should have worked for you. You should have written a bestseller by now and something way better than *Naked Grapes*. What the fuck. Weren't you working on something before your appointment at the clinic? Because that's what we fucking thought."

"I'm sorry. I'm sorry about it all, I can't write still and about the smell up there. I'm embarrassed. But it's not me. It's that leopard! It gets hot with no AC and the leopard really stinks, like it's full honestly of fungus or honestly dried-up vomit. I have a hard time sleeping near it, but when I've attempted to put it out, she — "

" — Maron."

" — yes, Maron. She returns him to my room. She says she's capitulated about me being in the second bedroom but there's no way the leopard has to live anywhere else. She's so attached, but why doesn't she want it in her room?"

I was whining — going on. I liked talking with Alix.

"Maron is a survivor of a leopard attack, she never said?"

"Maron, she doesn't talk to me. We have hardly any communication. Sometimes I'm in the kitchen and she's in the kitchen and nothing happens. It's very degrading but it's, I feel, one of the problems with polyamory. I'm not part of it, on the calendar or whatever, so it's like I hardly exist to her. Polyamorers say they're about being more open to connection but they end up being closed off from anyone they're not going to ultimately fuck. It's honestly degraded me, maybe even more than my brain injury, to live like this in a greetingless house. What? She what?"

"She got attacked by a leopard. It opened up her back and took out a kidney, her spleen, and sliced open, too, her bowel. She's been through a lot, Cumin."

"Where was she?"

"Here. Philly. It had been trained by her father, a zoo worker, to hunt her down in Fairmount fucking Park where she'd set up in a tent, because he'd been well, Cumin, he had been fucking her. He let it out. He'd fed it her underwear and stuff. He wanted it to kill her, which it would have done but it was more, it started licking and nurturing her and hurting her and nurturing her, which she was used to in a way, this kind of fucking dynamic from waaaaay back. She was like Oh here we go. Maybe she didn't react as much as someone who hadn't been being repeatedly raped by her supposed protector since she was a fucking ten-year-old, so that helped. She kept her cool with the let-out leopard. And then some homeless dude axed its skull open where it was lying on her lap actually purring by the end of things, Cumin, if you can believe this fucking shit, though the axe got her shin as well but it was probably a good thing, because who knows how shit ends, best to put an axe in the ending, to split that leopard head before its right brain and left brain come together and collaborate on some humanities/STEM BULLSHIT that would really get her, plus it could have eaten her, but ultimately she's a beneficiary if you think about how the city, for employing her deranged raper of a dad, ended up paying out almost a mil, which isn't great but it's why she's got this fucking two-bedroom house with no AC even though she's just an artist. Or she was. Not that it excuses her from housing people in her fucking closet, Cumin, seriously, that's fucked, but you can see, can't you, there's this reason. Maybe she wants someone close by, maybe you didn't understand you were her protector, that she needed someone to, like, pay to protect her."

"I always thought it was through some sort of grant, like government assistance to help with your mortgage if you're an arts professional. Didn't she say that to you once?"

"I guess it's a *kind* of fucking grant, Cumin. But more like a MacArthur Genius Grant just in the fucking sense that you can't apply for this shit, you don't apply to be raped by your fucking dad. You have to be internally nominated."

"I didn't know all this. I'm sorry. I'll tell her I'm sorry."

"Whatever. It's no excuse. But it's interesting. That was the last thing she did, a one-woman show. It's a bit of a tiresome but also obviously sympathetic and affecting ninety-minute one-sided conversation with that stuffed leopard you think is more rank than your smoldering and exposed pussy during this exceedingly steamy summer, the Cumin Baleen summer of no underwear as I call it. The set is a tent in a city park system, but she'd do it every night in a bar — The Bar Noir — at the back of the bar."

"Did you see it?"

"It was put on before I knew her, because I'd met her at Moody when she'd quit the theater. But yeah, Cumin, she put it on for me in the basement. I asked her to. That was the night I came home with her for the first time, when you and I met."

"Oh."

"But yeah, that's all fucking over for Maron. She's retired from the theater. She said to me, 'The impulse to quit took root in me, and that became a compulsion.'"

"That's weird."

"Fucking why, Cumin? Of course she wanted to stop, after telling that kind of horrible story to a bunch of strangers every night. And they don't love you for it. People hate fucking victims. It was too much."

Something was off. He was fucking with me. I didn't want to say it, I didn't want to break the spell, a conversation, a kitchen, but I was aware, maybe you are, that it's what Day-Lewis said when he retired — "The impulse to quit took root in me, and that became a compulsion." — and also that his last film, *Phantom Thread* (2017), had overwhelmed both him and its director Paul Thomas Anderson with sadness.

"Was Maron's show a success?"

"There was a devastating review by Camille Paglia, since you ask. I'm sure that was the reason she fucking quit. Paglia teaches in the city, so you'll find her sometimes around, it's fucking strange. She seems so New York. Remember her conniptions over Sontag? Susan told a TV reporter she'd never even read Paglia, so Paglia, in 1993, went fucking ballistic in a TV interview, saying of fucking course Susan Sontag had read her, 'people have been mentioning me to her for *years* now, not only that but she can't continue to claim she's a bibliomaniac when she'd been living in New York and my book had been a bestseller in New York for years, etcetera, etcetera, etcetera.'

"'You know,' she said, 'Susan Sontag was an enormous figure

to us in the '60s, and, um, it's really unfortunate what she did to herself, you know, it's too bad because she was once a prophet of popular culture, then Sontag became very snobbish, and began chasing after all these male European writers and so on and she lost the cultural centrality that she had. *I* am the Sontag of the '90s, there's no doubt. Sontag belongs to the generation before World War II. She doesn't watch TV, she doesn't listen to rock, and she has been, uh, passed. Sontag is gone!' Paglia is very tough, Cumin, look at what she said about Sontag, and in her review she said about Maron that 'She's dull, OK, she's boring, she's solipsistic, she knows nothing about contemporary life, she's not a very good writer, OK.' It was in the *Inquirer*."

"OK."

"There was no fucking sympathy for what had happened to her from Paglia at all. Paglia made it sound like rape affords women the opportunity to exercise their narcissism."

"Is Maron's family still around? Did any of them see the show?"

"Her father was found OD'd on heroin in the leopard's emptied travel container, and he was using, Cumin, one of those big fucking zoo balloons, deflated as SHIT, as a tourniquet to do drugs, but Paglia was not taken in by any of this. Camille Paglia tore into Maron. She took the other fucking kidney. She said she wished the leopard had fully killed this little fucking victim. And she said the ending of the show was really just ridiculous."

"She didn't like the ending?"

"Well it's hard to end this shit. Maron's pain is fucking endless. You should be feeling so bad for her, Cumin. You probably should apologize, and, you should write us that sample. Are you writing anything at all lately?"

"How did she end it?"

"In the tent she's been telling her story, about all of the rape from her father and also her brothers, Cumin, to this fucking leopard who's attacked her and she's bleeding out, but who is also really listening to her, letting her say anything she wants to in between the attacks. She's willing to be eaten, if listening's in the mix."

"Does she die in the show?"

"No, Cumin, she doesn't fucking die. There's blood, it's red wine and she's basically throwing jugs of it at everyone like it's Blood SeaWorld though no one signed wavers or anything, they had to be genuinely surprised by that."

"So maybe Camille Paglia had come to the show wearing white cashmere or whatever."

"Cumin. Get fucking real. Have you ever seen Camille Paglia? She doesn't dress like that."

I remembered her from Jason Miller's performance. I'd seen her. She'd worn the cashmere.

"You're right, Alix."

"Paglia *hated* what happens next."

"What?"

"Maron starts eating mushrooms that grow for real in fucking Fairmount. They're a little poisonous, not too bad. But in the amount she eats — and she's eating it up — they made her vomit all over the leopard, every night at the bar when she performed this. She got really sick but she told me, at Moody, she tells me now, she kind of liked it, Cumin. She secretly *liked* it. Isn't that nuts? She liked getting sick and someone from the audience would inevitably get up and try to help her out and she liked that a lot. She'd black the fuck out. She doesn't even remember how any of her shows ended. It's kind of a big gift she gives herself, to just black out or anyway be totally fucking incapacitated for the denouement. Maron, who is always so responsible, and fashionable, Cumin, she's so fashionable her life is fashion, she's so beautiful, but she stopped being in fucking control. Isn't that amazing?"

"This is what Camille Paglia hated, the vomit?"

"Paglia was very turned off by this fucking shit. She took it as just another plea for a woman to be babied in our fucking society. Her review was like I wish those mushrooms would build up in her raped body and kill her one night. I'd come back to this unbearable performance just to watch this baby die. But I'd also, she said, Cumin, accept it if our little victim over here would leave fucking town. Just leave. Get out of Philadelphia, you know? Why not leave Philadelphia altogether? Who needs this in fucking Philadelphia? That's basically what the review was saying. Like, We don't need this trash, this leopard attracter and also, you know, this *rape attracter* here in our city, it's not even that bad what happened to you, you got in, what, one little leopard attack? You got in this one fucking fight, and your mom got scared so you're moving with your auntie and uncle to Bel Air."

Carbon Balloon

"I'M AT ULTIMO."
"I'm here."
"I talked to Alix."
"I had to get out of there."

This woman I sat down with at Ultimo wanted to talk with me.

"I had *always* believed," she said, "Carrie Bradshaw was a survivor. It made *sense* to me. She acted that way. In the first seasons *especially* she was throwing her stuff at people and walls. She would throw things at her best friends. She slammed chairs and threatened to upend tables, disrupting the other diners and damaging upscale NYC restaurant property, like, in almost every episode especially in the first few seasons. The late '90s. It was packaged as *passionateness* — the passion of Carrie — but I don't know I always *knew* there was some person at the writing table who was steering this ship from the root of their childhood rape. That's how the show read to me.

"Not even her, they weren't leaving *her*. She got upset in this, such an unhinged way. If someone *moved* to leave. To leave her apartment that *cesspool* of silk heaps, even if for an *hour*. To go *get* something. Like a coffee or going to *work* or to see some of their own family members. *It would begin.* Her very ferocious behavior. She was upset. Really disappointed and furious *all of the time*. It was unnerving to me. Her attachment style was that of an incest survivor. That's all. There aren't any parents (for the four good friends) on that show.

"A tell.

"Maybe that's how the writers met. They were from the same group. They were, I've imagined, in a *group* together and after telling their tales of rape and coercion and being disbelieved and so alone and as kids, and crying in the meeting place, they all started to group hallucinate about *a silk heap*, about Carrie — Carrie Bradshaw — C to the B — a C that staggers backwards to Before — being born from a silken and taffeta *nest* of clothes, a *taffeteria* in a really really big closet, big for the city I mean, as big as a city bedroom, and coming out so *formed*, horsey and adult and angry, not a trace of the old family around. Not a *whiff* of a mom or dad coming to visit, to see the city, the sights, to see a big play, or a brother, a cousin, no one from her high school, no one who could remember or who knew the parents, the father, or who saw you like that, back then, like a bird on a cutting board, like a pig with her rectum in lights."

"What are you making?"

"This? I'm only knitting to be furious."

"Are you going through something?"

Her tea — an oolong she explained was a little too *pale* — wasn't *amazing*.

"Are you going to get anything?" I went up for a cortado.

She said she was using knitting to occupy her hands because she couldn't write any more — she had writer's block.

"You're a writer?"

"A *screenwriter*. I'm writing a screenplay but I'm stuck. I came here to knit. Look, I didn't bring my laptop."

I envied her nonmedical writer's block. If I had nonmedical writer's block, I thought, maybe I could write this sample. I looked at my little piece of paper and some of the sentences I'd written since arriving.

"I am cold."
"The mushrooms are off-gassing?"
"Something happened."

"I met one of the writers for *Sex and the City* (1998–2004) at a residency program. She was my tutor! They called them our tutors in a British way, they were very serious people. I became determined to find out if she'd survived incest. Maybe she — one of the writers — was the reason CB was such a survivor."

My tablemate *looked* like SJP but semitic — *oliven* — everything that's pale, or pink, it's a no, and instead she had brackish hair in the shape of a busted triangle, overstuffed and sprung, like a stabbed cushion. Gray tinsel was at 1/3 throughout.

She wore a long dress — in a reactively unfeminine shape — black and with a print of rusty triangles shmearing into spectrums, continuums and traces. I mothed about the pattern, overstaring into her dress even near the hot zones. I was being inappropriate. I tried to compensate by actually listening. I couldn't, though, find the triangle I really wanted, I couldn't peel off triangles with my eyes alone and put them on my zones and use the rotations of Earth in friction with constellations to make them vibrate like madeleines, so I kept staring and trying to really listen.

"The *Sex and the City* writer was my third choice. I wanted to work with a *woman*, and she was one of three. In a way she was my *last* choice, the last woman. There were about forty tutors to choose from, from a menu. I paid a lot I mean of money."

"Who was the most famous?"

"The Coen brothers. It's a big scene. But a lot of people were like me, trying to get in with women, who weren't as famous, though *Sex and the City* is prestige for TV, and the tutor had worked on *Sex and the City 1* (2008) and *2* (2010) as well. They go to Dubai?"

"Nobody thought men could be their mentor? I'm sure a Coen brother could help you out . . ."

"No they were very aloof. Very gregarious and aloof."

"Do you wish the show — or the *Sex and the City* movies — had talked *openly* about the incest Carrie Bradshaw had survived?"

"Are you talking specifically about the elevators in *The Shining*? Blood coming out of them in the hotel lobby?"

"Something like elevators, sure. Blood coming from her compulsive closet or something. Did your tutor ever confirm it? I don't know how else to ask. Was the tutor a surv...?"

"I think maybe a Coen brother *could* help, I mean maybe they really might. I don't know. It's more, and this seemed to be the feeling among the women who were the primary customers of this sort of pricey residency I did — let me explain. It was at this Catskills resort and farm where *Dirty Dancing* (1987) had actually been filmed. It was tailored for women like me, born in the '80s, Jewish, for whom that all *meant*.

"Men aren't *good* at screenwriting, Cumin. They've made good work through the torsions of industry, there are good producers, and of course great actors, and we like it, we like those movies, I personally like *Burn After Reading* (2008) from the Coen brothers. I *like* the fuck chair genre."

Had I told her my name?

"I like Claire Denis's film *High Life* (2018) for the same reason, when Juliette Binoche in that film and in her 60s at this point goes into that room on the spaceship where there's a *fuck chair*, and she undoes her braid and it looks like river webs, like a map of a witched earth, on her strong back... I like the figure of the movie director as the inventor of the *right* fuck chair, and that was the right fuck chair for Binoche or her character or whatever in that moment, I like the moment in a film where someone opens up a door and there's a fuck chair, or in *Burn After Reading*, where the fuck chair, George Clooney's *pride*, is in the basement of his DC townhouse. All ready to go."

I didn't know what to believe. I knew that *Dirty Dancing* was set in the Catskills but filmed, actually, in North Carolina, outside of Asheville. I'd been there, to a residency *there*. I tried to imagine a fuck chair scene in that meaningful film, *Dirty Dancing* — a fuck chair in a recreational barn, a fuck chair in the corner, or in a room with an abortion in progress, fucking that doctor who turned out to be like a butcher. A bad doctor — "The guy had a dirty knife and a folding table."

"I seem to remember *Dirty Dancing* wasn't filmed in the Catskills at all!"

"In the film, Cumin, there's no farm, but actually at the real *Dirty Dancing* resort in the Catskills, it is *mostly* a farm, with a lot of animals, but the thing that men, or male screenwriters I mean can't do, is they don't really write *rapport*.

"Their scripts are very *lean*, Cumin.

"If I tried to get mentorship for my screenplay, which is a thriller, these male mentors would end up talking to me about *pacing*. They'd emphasize pacing to me. Can you imagine. They'd want me to write something at a lean pace like something is *gaunt*. Something is moving because it's starving — it's gaunt. That's good screenwriting to these butchers and they'll put montage music over the conversations to keep things nice and lean. A starving jaguar in a dead world. Hm. It's not accurate. There are jacarandas around the world.

"'Nice and lean,' they'd coach me making so much money on this stupid summer gig. They'd take the writing of rapport out! *Rapport* is important. Everyone needs rapport, money can't buy you rapport, you can't carry your watermelon across the Sahara all by yourself, you know what I'm saying to you?"

I thought of all the times — all the times — in my little life I'd been caught at the wrong table at a café. I thought our phones had eradicated most of these moments, these garish and ultimately worthless listening scenarios, all the things thrillers and dialogue in general can't capture, all the dialogue that's worthless to print, like this, and I thought, anyway, Ultimo would be closing. I'd be saved by its closing up around 9 p.m. But it was open late. There was something going on at Ultimo. More people kept coming in.

"But a thriller *should* be lean." — I tried to say *something* — "That's the whole point of genre. It tells you what to do in this ended place."

"There *is* rapport in a thriller."

"What's your thriller?"

"I went for a lot of walks with my tutor at the *Dirty Dancing* farm and resort in the Catskills. I could never get her to tell me, though, if she was an incest survivor. I tried to create an intimacy..."

"What did she have to say about your screenplay? Did she understand how to teach you to build any rapport?"

"We visited this *morbundite*."

"A morbundite?"

"A morbundite is a sleek, haunted donkey that comes from Belarus, it's not *donkenus* technically for the genus but it's genuinely, Cumin, like a donkey dragged through a mossy ditch of Daniel Day-Lewis–ishness, that's really the only way I can say it. A piercing animal. A sort of, a sex donk."

I thought of course of Maron and her Daniel Day-Lewis quality, which I could never have competed with. Alix had performed a fair amount of moral disgust over her housing me in the closet, but that was over. He came on Saturdays, there were others on the other days. Polyamory grinded on. Maron rarely said hello even when we were both in the kitchen. She wasn't hung up on anything. She'd put a big sticky note on the door — GET US THE SAMPLE.

"Why were there morbundite?"

"*Morbundites*. It's not like deer. It's plural. There was only one morbundite, Cumin. Because of their known viciousness. Only one per a hundred acres, or so. That's the guideline. Otherwise it's very upsetting."

She showed me a picture of the morbundite she'd met and it did look sexy for a donkey, like it was, in fact, about to mouth the word *cognac*, as Daniel Day does, mouthing "cognac" with his fixed, his twinkling eyes, he mouths *cognac* in *The Unbearable Lightness of Being* to his country waitress, Juliette Binoche, in that movie. She brings one right over to him.

"I think I've heard of morbundite meat, isn't there a Bourdain on that?"

"We'd eaten some sausage made out of the last one. But he — the present morbundite — was a teenager, we were never going to eat him. The morbundites, they call out. It sounds like *cognac, cognac* all through the night. You could hear him ordering his cognac through the vegetables and fences while you lay there in your very own *Dirty Dancing* cabin, mm. My god I wanted to bring him one. My tutor and I would talk about him endlessly, instead of about my thriller. She wasn't doing her job. We were both crushing on him. He was our donkey boyfriend. We pretended to be jealous of one another over how he would look at us. Piercing, twinkling. *Cognac, cognac*. He was all hot, that was for sure. He would come out of his gate, slinky and limber, and follow us both around. We parted at the cabins, her to the staff side, with the other esteemed tutors, with the Coen brothers and David Cronenberg, and Brandon Cronenberg, who were, I learned, having dance-offs over there that us customers couldn't dream to compete in, really high-level, and slutty, even between father and son, scissoring, and when we parted, me and my tutor, our boyfriend would turn back to his area, ambling. He had tight balls, with no hair around them. One day he did choose me, only a little. He followed me about three feet toward my cabin, and then he turned and ambled away.

"That was *it* between us. She never spoke to me after that, though we had a week left and I was paying to work with her. *Very* Carrie Bradshaw. She was feeling the deep turmoil of that slight and *bestial* rejection. Huffing at her laptop in the dining area, putting on a show sitting there at night in a big overblown ball gown, smoking though you weren't allowed, so upset about this slightest of slights, from our fucking fake morbundite boyfriend, he wasn't even ours, he wasn't human, he was, what was he, he was just a little piece of premeat, Cumin, but she felt so so abandoned, but she was no Carrie Bradshaw. My tutor was a really hideous woman."

"I thought Carrie Bradshaw was a gay man on the inside, I thought that is the secret inside of Carrie, the gay man — not necessarily the story of a hideous woman and her incest."

"She was disgusting. She looked like a fuck chair abandoned in a dumpster for, like, *a reason*."

The sun smashed its big dumpsters of Oranginas on the bricks of all the rowhomes across the street. It was setting. More late-night comers were pouring into Ultimo and an open mic event was seeming to be being set up. I'd seen a few of these in my days as a writer, as the author of *Naked Grapes*, back when my eyes had been but bubbles blown off the brain, how inaccurate. My tablemate told me at length the story of her thriller and I tried very hard to orange concentrate, but I couldn't.

I kept staring at the people and the open mic being set up, but it wasn't an open mic.

Oh no.

It was an MFA thesis reading for one person, a young man. A graduate of creative writing, here in a city of hospitals. He was going to read his thesis to all of us, for over half an hour. A little program was being passed around. It said as much. We were going to be treated to a "long short story."

Oh my god.

His parents were there. His professors.

I began to think of all the men I'd known who were pursuing creative writing, like recalling a series of bad dates I'd been on in Manhattan. The one with the scarf. The ass licker. The one with the agent. The raper. The argue-ist. The one writing a 9/11 novel. The one writing a rape scene from the perspective of the bed.

I shuddered. I said to my tablemate, "We should get out of here. Pronto. Do you live around here?"

"Cumin," she said, "Cumin Baleen. I thought you recognized me, this is why you wanted to *finally* talk. Aren't we both here for the same reason?"

The lights were dangerously dimming down!

"I *live* in Maron's closet. I moved in a week ago . . . I'm so sorry. I'm just out of eye surgery — something is really screwy with my brain. Tell me. Have I been going on and on?"

And just like that, it was too late.

A Manager

IN 2000 AT OCEAN CITY HIGH SCHOOL THERE WAS only one incoming freshman with a mohawk, and it was me. Most of the kids at Ocean City High were the grandchildren, children, or nephews and nieces of pissed-off contractors, still pissed. No other mohawks though.

What other students got into was far from my ideals. It was all frosted tips, parachute pants, Smash Mouth. Only when I showed up in the freshman class was there any difference. I wasn't linked to the area, jointed to family stories of a big building boom in the 1980s, and then bankruptcies. My mother was a doctor. Some of the older teachers would go on about being kids on the boardwalk, the fact that the older boardwalk was closer to the ocean and spray would come up through it and refresh their bare feet, their mothers would put rubber tips on their high heels so they didn't fall through. These teachers, with their hopeless nostalgia, were intimidated that my mother wasn't putting tips on her shoes — but was a urologist. I was an OK student, but right from the start of high school I got nothing out of it and spent my time getting subeducated by punk albums especially from the band Fifteen. Every afternoon of freshman year, after my nap in afterschool detention, I walked along the boardwalk up to Gillian's Pier and sat on a bench with my back to the water, listening to that band's latest album *Survivor*, eating two slices.

> *Maybe it's too many burgers maybe it's too much beer*
> *Maybe it's in the water maybe it's in the fear*

> *Maybe it's too much pollution maybe we are just dumb*
> *But it really seems to me that*
> *Americans are stupid*
> *We'll fall for anything and everything*
> *The only thing worse than a stupid American is someone who actually gets it*
> *And decides to do nothing*

Without making you feel that I was like one of those Columbine kids, souring on the normies and working myself up into unthinkable acts, I made a pact with myself to stay detached. I didn't have any trouble not socializing with the kids at school — I was a straight-edged celibate punk in a deeply private conversation with nothing but my Discman, and later books by Jeff Ott — Fifteen's front man — and Mumia, Jello Biafra, Assata Shakur, and Henry Rollins. The me who is writing today doesn't look upon the me of then, the prickly young punk, as having been especially homosexual. I'd like you to think back on your own adolescence. All bright teenagers are more or less devoid of sexual desire or are flooded with it but from all angles, a mix of genders, sea, sand, and stone — you could hold a glass, a waffle, and tremble, but needless to say, I out of everyone was the least surprised by 9/11.

On the first day of class after it happened, my sophomore year, the teacher came into the classroom with a slender kid, who wore glasses and a young budding mohawk, a Fifteen T-shirt loose on his frame. He stood beside her hanging his head straight down so I could see the firm, controlled green at the tips of each baby spike.

I turned to my tablemate, the blocked screenwriter. I shared sections from *The Sea and Poison* that I had pulled up on my phone.

> On the first day of class of the second term, when I was in the fifth form, the teacher came into the classroom with a small

boy, who wore glasses and had a white head band. He stood beside the teacher's dais hanging his head to one side like a girl, staring at a spot on the floor.

The MFA graduate lifted this from Endo, I had recognized his scheme — a scam? — from the moment he began reading! It was all an echoing, or a kind of syntactical mirroring, from a late section in *The Sea and Poison*: "An Intern." The chapter tells the personal history of Toda, a medical student who, unlike Suguro, feels *remorseless* about human vivisection.

> About 1935 in Rokko Elementary School on the eastern edge of Kobé, there was only one pupil with long hair, and that was me [...] Most of the pupils were the children of farmers. No lads like me with long hair.

How could this graduate have known such a reader, a rereader, of *The Sea and Poison* would be at Ultimo? He stood there reading his long short story to us. His hair was long and so damp even now from a shower. I could see just the way he'd dealt with his writer's block, and with a thesis due ...

"Everyone," this young teacher in a costume-ish business suit said to us in her voice designed to barge through dreaming, "here's someone specially impacted by recent events who has moved here to live with family friends. Give him your most caring treatment. Otherwise you are not a patriot."

Then someone called out to him, "What is that, your age?" After all this was a homeroom for sophomore students at Ocean City High, many of us in the room were aged fifteen. To wear such a shirt just at this moment was a bit like wearing a shirt with your name on it.

"You, Matt, can Sören shadow you for the day?"

There was commotion in the classroom, the teacher obviously typing us together with our hair, black clothes, slender bodies. I looked at the guy, his eyes broad on his face and washed blank, with a feeling more or less of jealousy. Here was someone who presumably had lost his family.

"Don't be naïve about Endo, Cumin," my tablemate had replied. Not quite whispering. "He was obsessed with Flaubert and the beginning of *Madame Bovary*. The figure of a new boy and his hair? It's all over the place. His chapter 'An Intern' in *The Sea and Poison*? It's lifted from the start of *Bovary*, when Bovary is a boy in school."

I'm looking it up.

> The "new fellow," standing in the corner behind the door so that he could hardly be seen, was a country lad of about fifteen, and taller than any of us. His hair was cut square on his forehead like a village chorister's...

The MFA student continued: As the new boy was now to be my shadow, I took him to my English class. "Everyone, I've asked you to journal some of your thoughts and feelings about what happened," this same teacher from homeroom reminded us. "Sören, you don't need to participate in any of this and you can leave the room if you want to. Matt do you have yours?"

To see my English/Homeroom teacher behave with compassion to another punk was a blow to my self-esteem. I had thought she'd dismissed me because of my hair and clothes, but now saw that it was something else, demeanor or manner, a spirit in me she didn't like or couldn't be gentle with.

I took out my class journal and began to read what I'd written for the assignment of reflection. I always enjoyed reading out loud. To feel my throat grow course with the knots and kinks and grab bars of my own ideas was a good sensation, but for this reflection I'd written a mask. The smell coming off the new student seated next to me affected me. He came from New York.

His mohawk was immaculate; he smelled of a very pure peanut butter. He'd painted his shoes.

"I don't want to read this in front of him," I thought to myself.

When I wrote my reflection on 9/11, I tried to make it sound dumb and typical. I wasn't sociopathic exactly, but if my goal were to shore up my energies for real change, it would be wasteful to perform actual critique, or real grief, before this teacher in particular, who had read to us aloud selections from *Tuesdays with Morrie* (tearing up) and who (going hand in hand with that) passionately encouraged us to submit to the annual *Atlas Shrugged* Essay Contest. ′strong surges of patriotism and fear that were everywhere abounding using a series of imploring, mournful, and building questions, in an exhortative rhetorical style promoted by Longinus, which precluded my knowledge of a) the School of the Americas and b) the real terror that never gets addressed by government like domestic abuse, rape, starvation, and drug addiction, because solving them would lift up poor people, Black people, and women.

I began to read aloud in front of everyone. So much was humiliating now, in front of this Sören. As a special nod to this teacher, I'd lifted text directly from my mom's copy of *Tuesdays with Morrie* and had played a kind of MadLibs with the sentences, bending each one to somewhat be on the topic of the recent tragedy, knowing she'd be soothed by the very syntax of that syrupy stuff. I told, instead, of an imagined visit with *her*, who, deeply trembling with the pain of the tragedy, submits to *me* her wisdom about these new terrifying times, how to take heart and so on. Finally it was done. When I saw the expression on her face, I felt a sense of relief that she had been touched, oblivious to parody.

"Sören, tell us any reflections you have about Matt's reflection."

"I think that Matt is processing a lot of necessary emotions right now, and that's good."

"I couldn't agree more, Sören, thank you, and I hope that —

you know that — I hope that it didn't hit home — I hope that you know that — "

Seizing her chalk our teacher began to write on the board. She wrote the word *healing*.

"When Matt was reflecting on the tragic event, he felt a mixture of grief and anger, and fear, and that's just the way he wrote it out. Many of you try to shield or mask your emotions in your journal entries. But Matt has written exactly how he feels. That's the way to *heal*."

This was the way I had decided to act whether at school or at home. And by doing so, I preserved myself for a coming life of life — I chose distant interlocutors over the milieu at hand.

I stole a sidelong glance at the new mohawked guy, who, his nails painted a hardy purple, was staring, too, at *healing*. Did he feel me looking? He rotated his head with its hard and precise spikage and looked at me. For a few moments we looked at each other. He actually blushed, and a smile crept onto the pale scene of his gorgeous face.

"You fooled them all, eh? I see you." His cute smile seemed to be telling me just this, and I could see in his face, and the way he was nodding, that he was singing to me silently something from the band Fifteen, something Ott had taken almost verbatim from Hendrix (my mom had pointed it out, the one time I forewent headphones).

> *White-collar conservative businessman*
> *Point your plastic finger at me-e-e*
> *Soon my kind are gonna drop away and die*
> *But I'm gonna wave my freak flag HIGH*

I looked off. I could feel the blood, the blushing, beginning. Voices from the choir room, a cappella, leaked over with a gush of ocean wind:

That saved a wretch like me!

Sören and I got together, we started working together at the pizza place Mack & Manco's, we hoarded pies to take under the boards, with fresh needles from my mom's office and blankets for homeless kids, we projected a map of Palestine onto *Saving Silverman* at the Moorlyn Theater.

He had nobody really. During winter break he moved to my house. During Hanukkah, while I lit the menorah with my mom, his still-growing spikes wavered in the doorway. When we went out later to leave our gifts on top of trashcans for homeless teens, he made me promise, "Always give everything away, if you didn't scrap it, steal it, or make it" as he put on the rim of the trashcan the Ray-Bans my mom had got him, and a box of Godiva chocolate, too. I would have, I thought, liked to see him wearing those glasses, but it was sexy, too, to see how he left them there, the angle of his giving, purging wrist. We drove to Wildwood and got matching tattoos, the numbers 15 huge on our hairless sternums and the letters J and O, for Jeff Ott, on the tops of each of our feet, which was fucking hurtful, so now each of us, two punks, were like walking triangles, and even now I can feel the pull of the rusting wire that connects my chest to each foot, and binds my feet in a pact of purpose, and I still hear the music from that *Fifteen* album:

I refuse to believe God created me
To be abused

Then he was with the recruitment officers. I was gonna leave the school building early to go help this kid who was setting up a detox floor in his punk house in Philadelphia when I saw Sören with two other guys getting loaded up on literature and writing out their numbers and emails on these cards the ROTC officers put in a metal box that had a lock. He shook the officers' hands.

Our old English teacher — Ms. Pattat — was with him, and I stood there and watched her hug him for a few moments.

"Are you leaving the school building, Matt!"

I shook my head, trying to show her I was only outside to get some sun.

When Sören and our homeroom teacher came near, I could see their faces were red. Sören stood behind her a little.

"Matt, you know this is a closed campus — you can't come and go even if you have a free period."

As Sören raised his face in the sunny, salty air, the light lit it up and caught his extreme paleness in a hold of egret.

"What, you still want to fight? Even though it's not even gonna be in the right country?"

I began to cry. Our teacher was now standing beside me with her hands on my shoulders.

"You won't be 'on reserve' for long!"

"Now what is this about for you, Matt?"

"Ms. Pattat, he ... Sören over here ..." I blubbered. "He thinks he can change the system from within it but he's mistaken."

Sören moved to our teacher's condo near the bay. When we were back for spring semester, she would bring him in her car, a knit hat on his head, in his ROTC outfit. She wrote on the board in homeroom one February: Weapons of Mass Destruction.

"What is the stuff? Does anyone know?"

No response from her or anyone.

"Sören?"

"It's anthrax. It's that and other biological agents like botulinum toxin, aflatoxin, and ricin."

"Iraq has produced four tons of a deadly nerve agent called VX. Did you know that a single drop of it on your skin will kill you in minutes? So now imagine there are four tons of it waiting to be put into rockets, into chemical shells."

In moments like this our homeroom teacher became one and

the same with Colin Powell, like she'd had that UN speech memorized. And me, I thought about all the kids that were about to die because Colin Powell showed the world a vial of powder, because of a trace memory of anthrax from the sad, disorienting days right after 9/11, because who blew up building 7, though, and I thought Sören was crazy.

"Matt, why don't you on behalf of the class write a reflection on Sören's leaving," said this teacher when he was called up from reserve, predictably right after his graduation.

He shared a last shift with me at Mack & Manco's. Our manager always wanted us to know that how they used to do it was they had a hose full of sauce they'd turn on over the dough, the pies were going so quick, and everyone would come and watch, when he was a kid in our shoes, but we didn't care about white nostalgia, and I was a vegan and didn't even feel so great giving it out for free, when we stole it, when I stole it, when Sören couldn't steal any longer like being ROTC was joining some kind of Eagle Scout type organization, as if the Boy Scouts wasn't about raping little kids, as if stealing were the wrong thing here, and I really felt, in that moment, there wasn't much I wouldn't steal, smash, or kiss, so I did lick him on his cheek.

For a while I'd calm down a panic attack looking over my tattoos. His brothers in the army would ask him about them, I thought. They'd sneer "What is that, your age?" And then it finally occurred to me that J and O, on his two feet, were also the initials of his killed father, Joseph Oeda, so he'd tricked me, he'd had a backup or a forefront meaning that was nothing to do with me, or being a punk, fifteen being his age when his father, Joseph Oeda, not Fifteen's front man Jeff Ott, was killed, which is about the time I realized he didn't even go to Iraq because he thought he could change the system inside of the system, whistleblow or release documents or something, that he must have wanted bloody revenge.

The college I entered was Blue Bluff University, inland thirty minutes into Galloway, New Jersey. Commuting in my mom's old Camry three days out of the week, I prepared for a BS in Social Work, largely by shuttling myself through a diffuse core curriculum, which gets topped off, right at the end, with a six-week practicum at some local clinic. On my drives Songs: Ohia's *Didn't It Rain* showed me that *perilousness* becomes a fortitude if you give it a tune —

> *If the blues are your hunter*
> *Then you will come face to face*
> *With that darkness and desolation*
> *And the endless endless endless endless endless endless depression*
> *But you are not helpless*
> *You are not helpless*

Social Work majors were divided into several core specializations, according to our interests, I wanted to work with addicts. In this interest I completed core coursework in biomedicine, ethics, composition, and communication studies. It wasn't that I neglected my studies to any great extent, but rather that my memories reaching out to homeless youth under the boardwalk in Ocean City, and then in Wildwood, where there were more, and later working at the detox punk house in Philly, in Kensington pretty close to 2100 North American Street in Fishtown where Jason Molina recorded *Didn't It Rain* in 2002, when I was fifteen, dwarfed my impression of the peer-reviewed articles I was assigned, and I thought, at least in high school that clamp of ideology was more openly sadistic, more openly wanting of me, but here, at Blue Bluff, professors and administration were impervious, confident, gentle, and distracted. In short, I began to believe in knowledge transmitted by one-on-one interaction, a connection inside of the pureness of crisis, and I wondered at the way *Tuesdays with Morrie* had been my secret seed, surprise bible, the tutelary text which would help me, ultimately, not hold out for that prize practicum at the end of the relentless core curriculum. I ended my studies.

Jason Molina put out a new album in 2009. I decided to see him play at the Trocadero in Philadelphia. I was deepening my work in Kensington where we had a needle drop-off and people could try to detox with us, basically in sleeping bags on Benadryl. I went on some weekdays and was considering moving into the house, leaving Mack & Manco's for good. I had a conviction that the surest way to help those who are sick, with incurable broken hearts, with incurable disease, would not be through my mother's medical system. Then, too, while I myself was not an addict, addiction seemed to me all that was appropriate, and at this point I was identifying as a sex-abuse survivor.

At the Troc, I found Molina playing one of his last shows before he'd retreat to rehabs, then that Christian goat farm in West Virginia, and die trying to *heal* —

Try-y-y to beat it
Try-y-y-y to beat it

My mother was this doctor; my stepfather, my rapist, also practiced medicine. So I decided I didn't want to be around a real clinic. Rather, at the punk house, I had a good way, a good sleepingbagside manner, a good feel for giving out doses of Benadryl or herbs, a feel for the limits of each new person's body, like, when to stash them in my Camry and jet to the ER.

Back at Blue Bluff, I found ornithology. I spoke at length with my professors about local preservation of salt marsh, the most productive land on Earth. An ornithology professor went by his first name, Alix. He took us out there, to the refuge, in his old pants and rubber boots. He told us how this stuff is like a buffer to the upland coastline for hurricanes, and was feeding grounds for ducks, geese, herons, and egrets. Not much was even capable of growing in a marsh, a few plant species that's it. But it's *still* the most productive. My vegan heart pounded! I was technically in my junior year at this time, supposedly preparing for a senior practicum, but I registered for unrelated classes boasting of field trips. Alix made us all drink tea with him, pouring this very spicy peppermint tea out of his big thermos into our little styrofoam (sorry) cups, like he was mamma and we opened up our big squeaking styrobeaks all around him, and we walked down the viewing boardwalk at the marsh not saying anything.

I liked this so much better than the beach, than *that* boardwalk. The class was fully enrolled with thirty of us who had arrived to the refuge in Blue Bluff vans, and even in my junior status I stayed out of eye contact with everyone on the first day, too shy, wanting to spot birds, sure, but using birds, too, as a looking-elsewhere excuse, why I genuinely did not know he was there, maybe had been in my van, when he walked right next to me. Sören.

"Those martins, when they come out of their gourds, are gonna be fantastic don't you think?" He shrieked and ran to the front of the students, where we moved en masse as a shy stumbling group, some of whom I learned later had never had tea before, and didn't know how to drink it or what it was for.

As he stopped, waiting for me to catch up to him ahead, he elegantly drank his tea.

As to be expected, once his training was over, he'd went to Iraq immediately, joining a group going to Baghdad. The sunset ruminated inside of the military plane and he watched the ocean below dissolve the whole disjointing marigold hologram (the sun) on its ruddy, burlapping tongue. The base was hot. His footsteps turned toward the long, immaculate bathroom. He sat on the toilet. By some extraordinary chance, his only parent had been killed in 9/11, the circumstances were such. But Bush had wanted to invade Iraq since the moment he was president, Sören knew that. Sören now thought: In 2001 2,996 Americans including Joseph Oeda died of terrorism; but in any case so did 30,622 of suicide, and anyway 71,372 of diabetes. What was he doing here? He should be helping people who have diabetes, so he was here at Blue Bluff, he told me in the van on the way back, doing a certificate in urban agriculture and food systems or something. But what did he do to get out of Iraq?

"I played Dungeons & Dragons for a year. I became a great Dungeon Master. There were a lot of guys there who wanted to play."

When I went back to class a week later, the students were talking about something.

"Poor Alix. I wonder who's gonna teach us now."

"No kidding! He's not coming back! What happened?"

I felt my face stiffen despite myself, and I looked around for Sören.

"I guess he brought around his boyfriend or something, no one who was enrolled. Did you see who?"

"Who?"

"Some guy who's not even registered. They got into a fight in the parking lot and the campus cops had to break them up. They were fist fighting each other, but that guy had been with us on the trip!"

"It was such a nice day" — the students yakked, the initial awkwardness of being in a new class dropped at the spice of gossip — "what could have made them so pissed off?"

"It seems they'd been living together for a couple years, a serious couple."

"What f_____s!"

The next semester, in the fall, I reported to my practicum. In front of Oceanside Surgery & Medical Center, I saw him walking in with Alix, who looked half-dead in a wheelchair.

As I passed with my new supervisor, I could hear their voices checking in at the desk. Within an hour, it seemed Alix was going to have a tumor taken out of his leg.

"I know that guy back there. I took a class with him!"

"He'll be taken care of, Matthew. This is a first-rate place for the most serious of procedures."

"I didn't know. I thought it was a lot of cosmetic stuff or something."

The rehabs I had requested to do my practicum with had refused, and all the other practicums started vanishing. Even worse, my mother forced Oceanside to take me, seeing as this is where she worked on her prostates.

I didn't think of myself as a person whose conscience was being compromised. I was disappointed my practicum was turning out to be another managerial position with more in common to my work at Mack & Manco's then my time at the Kensington detox house, but I felt an interest in routine, localism, in finally making friends. It so happened that after graduation when I moved from practicum to assistant manager for billing and coding under the agreement I'd concurrently work toward a 9-month certificate in billing/coding from Devry, with Oceanside paying, a lot of awesome people started working at Oceanside. For the first time, I had a circle of friends.

We all ate lunch together. We hopped over to the AC boardwalk, got slices, and sat even in our work slacks on the sand, though someone usually brought a big towel we'd sardine in on, and one time for a premeditated group dare we all stripped to bathing suits and plunged in the water, on a 30-minute break, and came back to work dripping. My feeling for making the world a place more worth living in didn't go away but it moved onto a more personal, discrete plane.

I went out with my coworkers — other new managers, coders, people working at check-in or security, or in the lab, some cute young male nurses — after work, to Ducktown Tavern with its flashing sign of a big gangsta duck out front chomping on his cigar, where I always ordered Asian Salad with the fried chicken strips removed onto a side plate.

"Why don't you eat meat? If you don't eat that or cheese or eggs or anything, how are you getting enough protein or fat?"

"I eat a bag of avocados a day, dude." Even with Ducktown's big TVs playing four kinds of sports (with sound) and a jukebox that was open game, I could follow everything a nurse, Ethan, was saying.

And I could also hear his cute little breaths and swallows, of his Diet Coke, as well.

"I'm fed up. I'm just fed up."

He told me of some of the nasty tricks he saw doctors doing, when they wrote out their records for different surgeries, to rack up the insurance money. He sighed deeply, and began retying up his longer, scraggly hair. Bedhead guy. Lean but looking like he'd lifted patients right up, a muscle guy in the nursing biz, someone who can easily roll, lift, or plant a patient on a toilet all day long. Scraggly, lean, strong.

"What a life! Do you like seeing people at their worst, needing so much?"

"It's not like that. People who get surgery are superdignified, they are actively and like literally *holding it together*."

That night my mom came to my room venting again, they'd canceled a full slate of her surgeries for some guy, he wanted all her ORs to use as his recovery rooms, overspill. So until about ten o'clock, I'd sat down with her and went over the table showing which doctors used which ORs, the schedule. Then in the middle of the night, I heard her crying.

"Don't tell anybody. I want you to start tracking how many surgeries this guy does each week. You know it's inordinate. It's way too many."

That morning, I looked through the number of surgeries I'd been helping to bill for that doctor at the center.

"Matt, we're all going to Ducktown." My friend Steven, in security, let me know. He usually went home to his family so this was not a night to miss.

"If you're going, I'll be there."

So, I went, but sitting there with Ethan I said to him, "Wanna go across the street with me?" The group of us had trudged in our work clothes and work backpacks up toward the boardwalk more or less together, some people on cell phones negotiating time out with their partners, or getting them to come out, or shouting at someone, doing some wild whining, saying "fuck you" and stuff, and then, we'd stumbled into Ducktown before the place totally filled. Half of us were at a table, the other half poured in different places around the bar, which is how Ethan and I became a pair. Across the street was a very astute-looking oyster house.

"Have you ever been in here? This is marvelous!" Ethan rejoiced at our little getaway. Live piano was coming from the back of a gracious room with mahogany bar sort of thing. We sat there. Ethan ordered a plate of oysters, he said I *had* to. I squirmed and downed these suckers. Honest to God it felt like eating little clots or fermented evening bags of the sea — in fact when Ethan was in the bathroom I ordered more oysters and, surprise, a crabmeat cocktail. The pianist was making fun, playing elegant renditions of Morisette's "You Oughta Know" forcing us all, who were nostalgic and free, to sing out:

> *'Cause the joke that you laid in the bed*
> *That was me and I'm not gonna fade*
> *As soon as you close your eyes, and you know it*

I have no idea if Ethan remembers this evening. In all probability, if you add up the numbers of nights, and people in general, he doesn't. But at any rate up to the day I left, when I passed him in the hall at Oceanside, he didn't give a nod or smile or look or glance, so he either forgot me flatly, there's a lot of us, a lot of us oysters in the sea, a lot of things that feel pure, that happen, or he resented me and what happened.

I'd left with the piano player, someone I recognized from high school.

My lack of any urgent sense of responsibility for my mom's suspicions on Dr. Lacerta — what was its cause? My mom was my mother, not a doctor at Oceanside Surgery & Medical Center, not really, plus all the baggage of her marriage to that guy who came in my room, so it took my talking with Tanya. She was a nurse manager from the fourth floor (OB/GYN). I, a coding and billing manager, was almost always planted on the second floor. But I saw Tanya at an afterwork gathering at Ducktown and asked if she, too, thought Dr. Varan is an asshole — this doctor who'd been exacting with me. What flashed down on our conversation, though, was a depressing slab of details surrounding Lacerta, not Varan, and what *he* was doing.

If there had been any subtlety in the conversation, I might have missed it, a little tired, maybe groggy from being at work, being yelled at by Varan, seeing my mom suddenly near the bathroom. Tanya sat down next to me at our table, and with her hand on my arm, she laid it out. To make me see what he — Lacerta — was doing, she explained to me why women get hysterectomies, but in most cases you just give 'em hormones. She started explaining it to me, the kind of things you have to cut to get it out of there, how many things she'd cut, ligaments, or anyway she'd been watching, or handing over the instruments anyway, but a lot of these women didn't even know what was coming, and she was getting hysterical, her hand drenched and clamped down on me, one hand on my forearm, one hand on my knee, as if she were silently, grindingly, climbing me. She had been to Mary Beth. I told her I was supposed to go with this stuff to Cody. The problem of uterus stealing, as she put it, was not something that could go through Cody.

"They don't even know he's gonna take it out."

I moved to Sören's studio + kitchenette in Galloway. As my car pulled out of the complex's parking, Sören stood in the winter-burnt tree belt barefoot, waving and having coffee. It was a wet, foggy morning of early spring. As I drove off to Atlantic City, I must say that I began to sing to the radio. Then as I reflected a bit upon the suffering of so many at my place of work, I sang all the harder, opening all four of my windows all the way down, inviting the fog and the creeping fresh stink of a finally thawing-out ocean, first brine. The song went —

I am not writing about these experiences as one driven to do so by his conscience. I'm talking about precious moments; it's the precious moments, remembered, that will save us. But I look upon all of life as precious, the precious moments in my bedroom, my stepfather's precious visits, it's not that, he wasn't so precious, but isn't it, couldn't it be true — I felt it was, driving, in the zealous hold of Peter Gabriel — that each moment is a little laced with some tinsel, some trick, an egg, a door, what I mean to say is simple actually —

> *In your eyes*
> *The light, the heat (in your eyes)*
> *I am complete (in your eyes)*
> *I see the doorway (in your eyes)*
> *To a thousand churches (in your eyes)*

I, who knew a few things about direct action, activism, food, and not bombs — what would it mean to get Cody to listen to me, and what if that was too small, so whom do I disturb and who needs to know — how do I stop abuse?

There is something I would like to ask you. Aren't you, too, enmeshed in the programs and activities of criminals? Aren't we both witnesses to something? Haven't you, too, lived your life watching a series of things happen which you told yourself you weren't any real part of? Didn't you exonerate yourself because you feel like a child?

From my office on the second floor I was idly scrolling through the internet. Tanya and I were going to meet up later, and our duty, we'd determined, was to confront the VP, Hisbidus himself together, to hell with Mary Beth or goddamned Cody. Our confrontation that day would be a fierce one. In several weeks' time we'd poured all the dates into one Excel map of wrong; we color-coded the problematic patterns, I, wringing Devry for all that it was worth. Tanya was a swift pro. A nurse. Jason Molina had died.

Somebody had written on the internet that he'd died alone "with nothing but a cell phone in his pocket with only his grandmother's number on it." I learned later that Molina had been a big Luddite, knew his friends' numbers by heart — he had people. I didn't know it then.

I closed my office door. Tanya knocked for a while and then went up to confront Hisbidus herself — not good. I wrote out my resignation. That night as I lay in bed, I worried it was Sören in his sleep dying, needing help, but it was me, who was moaning, and I could not dispel these moans and groans until I turned on the light and sang, way out there, out of tune:

> *Did you really believe?*
> *Come on, did you really believe*
> *That everyone makes it out?*
> *Almost no one makes it out*
> *Almost no one makes it out*

Even this righteousness, of my resignation, which persists even now, is not one which brings any great joy. It seems a loss, my not attempting to talk to Hisbidus or the media.

And that's about it. When I called our old friends in Kensington they said they've become a nonprofit, they could use someone with at least a BS in Social Work. They said Sören could be a cook and we could live upstairs. In Kensington, I sit staring into the twilight of a muted TV while the residents (mostly) sleep and think:

"Will my heart trouble me with recriminations? We had, on our floors, a uterus stealer. He told them they had cancer."

I look up. Someone is at the door wanting to be admitted. We don't do it like this, in the middle of the night.

Those to Be Judged

EVERY DAY IS FOR THE THIEF.

When I was nineteen I made an appointment in the Midwest with an OB/GYN, to see about going on birth control pills. They'd asked if I wanted a woman but I said I didn't care.

The gynecologist put his thumb in my asshole. He said, "I like to surprise you."

In the present tense like that — *I like to surprise you*. He wasn't foreign, the grammar is there. *You*, he'd meant, as plural. All patients. In any case. I wasn't there.

Two women I know have been raped by their OB/GYN.

One of the women, she told me it had not occurred to her actually *for months*, that she'd been. When she called the office months later — with a new baby to look after — to say it had happened, to follow up in some way, she was told the OB/GYN left the practice. She never told anybody else besides a receptionist answering the phone, and she probably didn't even say it. She probably said, "I'm calling to make a complaint," and then she was just told, "He doesn't work here anymore."

She doesn't remember his name. She remembers it was a Jewish one almost sounding like ours.

The receptionist must have assured: "He isn't going to be back."

"But you didn't tell your husband? You had a husband? Where was he? He never came with you to these appointments?"

Her husband wouldn't have. I know him.

"You have to understand, Cume. I didn't *know* it was happening to me. It only occurred to me later."

This can't be *Heart of Darkness*, because it's just not. It's not a frame narrative much.

Heart of Darkness is a noted frame narrative, because of the narrator, Marlow, being an infamous bystander, not really, but at least compared to Kurtz, horrible Kurtz, beheading the people, using their heads as fence posts if you remember, Kurtz is the topic and Marlow moves toward and talks about the topic, but I'm not exactly on the outside of the topic (neither, really, is Marlow) because I was inside of this person when it had occurred.

"Don't worry," I'd been saying to her, in a conversation we were having over the phone before my second surgery appointment at the Moody Eye Clinic.

I was telling her, "I'm writing lately about the problem of gynecological rape."

"Oh?"

"Yeah, Mom. The problem of gynecology. There are cases all over the country, of rape, and about theft, too. Every day is for the fucking thief. Taking uteruses for no reason."

"What?"

"It's not like any of it is new. God. Now there are the big public cases, with George Tyndall at USC, Larry Nassar the pelvic-floor manipulating osteopath for the Olympian gymnasts, or Javaid Perwaiz, a uterus-stealing OB/GYN from Maryland. But they, all those men, had been doing this for decades, Mom, and one person, for example, who recently told me she'd been raped by her OB/GYN, she wasn't raped by Tyndall, Nassar, Perwaiz, or Amin — Mahendra Amin the uterus stealer working at the ICE facility — or anyone else in the *news*, or Robert Hadden in New York who raped pregnant women — *this was just her own discrete doctor*. If there are big cases, those are, in a way, nothing. Not nothing but they're the tip. The tip is flashing on, that's all."

"But it's all coming out only now, Cume. Nobody knew it was like this everywhere, not generally. It can't *generally* be this."

"There was a conference here at Penn in the '70s. A doctor divulged the contents of an unpublished report from the Department of Health, Education, and Welfare. One in five hysterectomies were being done for *sterilization alone*, OK. It's unnecessary."

I always talk to her like this, exasperated and teenaged. About anything. About cookies.

"These women who got those hysterectomies must have had something else wrong, Cumin. You don't know."

"To meet residency training requirements, interns at the time — maybe now, too? I don't know — these medical students had to perform an *amount* of hysterectomies. In order to get to that *quota*, what do you do, you do what you do, you persuade poor people who might have a tubal ligation or use *a condom* to instead get a full hysterectomy."

"You don't know that."

"Why because I read it? It's a quota — *a fixed minimum*."

"I know what a quota is — *God*. Don't be like this — didactic."

"These students are taking the Hippocratic Oath in their white coats of honor with fixed minimums in there, in the coats. Inner lining. It's like a stop-and-frisk policy for doctors, a frisk of the ute."

"Cume. Stop. *I know*."

"It's sick, Mom, it's sick."

"I never read about any of this happening..."

She'd asked me what I was working on. I'd called her from the waiting arena.

All I'd wanted to say to her was that I'd gotten it — her, childhood — out of my system, out of my writing literature system. Whatever were our problems, the sick family dynamic, the scapegoating. I was writing about other things now, entirely, because I was someone who reacts to the news, that's all.

I'm someone else, I seemed to want to say through the flip phone as I sat waiting for my second eye surgery.

"Don't worry," I'd told her, holding on to a withering ticket, "You're getting a break. It's not going to be about you anymore."
Naked Grapes, it was about patricide, fine, but it was about her.

A different person altogether had told me she'd been raped by her OB/GYN only a few weeks earlier. This woman had told me about it in a sports bar. I'd gotten the first surgery, one hole down, I remember, on December 26th. So I must have seen her before the second appointment, for the second hole in my iris, sometime right after the new year.

I'd had to — I was cornered — ask her if she ever had been raped.

Nassar's sentencing was playing on a mounted TV, by accident or by virtue of it being covered by ESPN. We were watching by incident the Olympic gymnast Aly Raisman, her being one of his hundreds of victims. She was wearing a hot pink blazer —

> You made me uncomfortable and I thought you were weird but I felt guilty because you were a doctor so I assumed I was the problem for thinking badly of you. I wouldn't allow myself to believe that the problem is you.

"Have you," I had to ask this woman, "been raped by a gynecologist?"

I felt cornered because this woman I was sitting with at the sports bar was really sobbing.

She had ordered a cosmopolitan, a drink associated with women and good friends who are out on the town together, but now it looked like a hoisted lake of Raisman's blazer, and she was sobbing a lot, drinking it up like someone down and out on *Sex and the City*, a show that depicts a rapeless cosmopolis.

"My mother stayed out in the waiting room. She thought she was affording me my privacy!"

Raisman said, "Each new day seems to bring a new survivor," and I felt we were really on the nose now, riding the nose like a centaur or Falkor through the air!

How do you ever get off of it?

We were meeting in the sports bar because it was convenient to Sea & Poison. She'd met me after my shift at nine. She didn't live in Philadelphia at all but was on a self-driven book tour, going to Barnes & Noble in Philadelphia, Pittsburg, Cleveland, and back to our arts college, where she now worked as an adjunct, to promote a memoirish self-help book she'd published on Amazon about the end of our friendship. No one was coming to these events, she offered, though she'd paid a special fee to get a list of contacts for Barnes & Noble managers all over the country, but she said many of the contacts were out of date and many people don't work at the chain for very long.

Jesus.

"What's with this city you're from?" she wanted to know. "It's a city of sports bars."

"We have no idea," said Raisman,

> just how much damage you caused, Larry, and we have no idea how deep these problems go. Now is the time to acknowledge that the very person who sits here before us now, who perpetrated the worst epidemic of sexual abuse in the history of sports, who is going to be locked up for a long, long time, this *monster* was also the architect of policies and procedures that are supposed to protect athletes from sexual abuse, for both USA gymnastics and the United States Olympic & Paralympic Committee.

"Damn," my friend said. "I kept seeing him. All through high school, and when I was home for breaks during college. I *asked* my mom to keep arranging those appointments. And you know, Cumin, I haven't gotten a Pap smear since I realized what was going on — that was over a decade ago."

"Damn," I said. We'd been friends when this was happening, I guess. But if she didn't know it how could I know? "Did you ever get Gardasil?"

"The vaccine?"

"If you're not getting checked out ever..."

"Uterine cancer? Cervical cancer?" she said. "I could care less," and I wondered in that moment if she was a suicide risk.

Suicide, you kill prevention.

Would I have killed myself? I was, at that very time, having so many thoughts.

I remember meeting the specialist, after the lab work came back the way it had. The bad blood. He'd said we could find the right medication for me. We would need to start with Plaquenil but keep trying from there. And, he put me — to cut the inflammation, the big pain — on some Prednisone.

Prednisone, I will meet you at the river.

Now I imagine meeting this specialist, or someone else, him or anyone in the profession, and I think, what if that doctor didn't say, "Let's find the right medication," or said it but raped me — maybe I would kill prevention.

I think about that. I can't help but wonder. About the iridotomy procedure, scam as it was, my angles not narrow, not being the worst thing in terms of medical scams.

I wonder, what if it saved me from sudden blindness, or the possibility of getting cataracts later on?

It was unfortunate how Raisman had come onto the TV just then, because the whole point of our meetup at the sports bar was to have a confrontation. But sometimes something flies in to soften or insane everything. She was wanting to give me a copy of her book, to finally tell me the big news, why she ghosted me over a decade ago. But then.

When I'd returned to the Midwest from Schipol, I'd seen her at parties or at galleries, or readings, and she didn't speak with me. Suddenly. Eerier than in NDiaye or Darrieussecq, because she hadn't disappeared. And I was there too. We were standing together. I said "hello" but it didn't work. "Hello" was a word that pumps wood into the blood of a friend. I pumped her full of hello-wood, I think I even screamed "hello," then left Chicago.

She was really sobbing still.

I never imagined we wouldn't be friends. My heart was like a Munchian jaw in the bar.

"Funny to think of a vaccine like that doing probably just as much work in preventing gynecological rape, if you don't have to get checked out as often. If you got Gardisil, you'd only have to get checked out every five years. You'd decrease your chances."

"Yeah," she sobbed. "I like that. We need a vaccine like that. For rape!"

"Sorry, Cume," my mom was saying to me as I sat at Moody weeks later, to get that second hole. I'd called her from the waiting arena to pass time. She continued: "I went to see my OB two days before you were born and he said I needed an exam. He put up a sheet so I couldn't see anything and no one else was in the room, which I thought was strange, and he was raping me. So. You are still writing about me. Isn't that something?

"But Cume, don't get me wrong. It's horrible. But I'm OK. You have to believe me. I didn't even realize he was doing it. I mean I was in a lot of pain, but I didn't understand it. I wasn't, in that way, a victim, no I wouldn't call myself that, because in a way I didn't even experience it."

I thought of my old friend who'd so recently told me something similar, that she'd been raped by her gynecologist. Was it even uncanny? Does this count as a coincidence? I'd met up with her only weeks before and sure, she had told me she'd been raped repeatedly as a teenager by her OB/GYN. Of course I thought of her! — they'd both been raped by an OB/GYN! I was wetting the surgical space of my waiting iris — and I laughed a little remembering what I'd told my old friend when she'd pushed that book at me, through her tears, with its embossed bubble of a stupid title, with its clip art of a big broken heel, I'd said, "I despise most publishing but can't bring myself to read anything self-published like this, that has not, I dunno, made out with a meatgrinder a little. This looks so pure, so dumb."

I guess I was really angry.

Cooking Without Cumin

MY NAME WAS CALLED AT THE MOODY EYE CLINIC.

How could I have defended her? I didn't know she didn't know she was being raped, and had I defended my own parent? Was I unborn and was I bobbing there inside while it was going on, without language or the air outside of her, and did *she* hate me for it?

I couldn't help but wonder, did she resent me for being such a useless bystander, *in*-stander, object in space, when she was raped but aren't we all so much the Marlow, don't we bystand in our own bodies in these spaces?

I wondered, aren't our eyes, if they've even opened yet, if we are afforded that grace before being introduced to the milieu of assault, only bubbles that are so sullen?

"Mom..."

They called for Cumin Baleen.

That's me.

So I got that second hole put into my iris, but the laser, the laser, for the second procedure I swear it went too far...

Immediately afterwards, if I went to work on my book, about gynecological malpractice, rape and uterus theft, this crisis in that profession, I found I wasn't able to make a sentence with more than one clause. I could research, I could read, and think in my way — What is oil? — but a sentence no longer had any copulatory frenzy, could not amass with discordance or pile with pleasures and problems, or enumerations of the things that *do* happen. I tried...

"I was with her."
 "What?"
 "What is oil?"
 "She went to the appointment alone."
 "I was there."
 "I love you."

In the Dickens archive (I'm looking at it now, in a special collections room at Penn) there's a play script that doctor, Helen Dickens, had been working on, "To Be a Great Black Woman."

Her archive includes her fastidious collection of articles, her evidence, research into problems in her own profession.

Her script's protagonist is an OB/GYN in a city of segregated hospitals, some of which wouldn't educate her — whose male students needed to be restrained when she graduated — so she's practicing in a private home in North Philadelphia in the 1930s. She says in the play about being a doctor, "I wish I knew so much more," which is not every doctor's prayer as some rely on what we can't imagine.

Fuck Chair

"YOUR FRAILTY, THIS *PLIANCY* OF POLYAMORY TURNS into your truth, that's all."

Mari's indicating how to climb in and out of his G-town mansion's attic if Captain — an old vocal instructor, almost dying — is out cold, post lunch. I can stow in it until I find a fitting situation.

I'm informing Mari now of my ostracism from Maron's post Carbon's taking up in my old walk-in. I told him, "Polyamory is running amok in South Philly!" though I don't know if Carbon is partaking. But I can't hark this, hour on hour. I can't hark Ruxpin — ugh — again.

I got a train.

"It's this way you polyamorous humans accord all your vigor to it, causing truths about your own cupidity, your salacity, to turn into an obligation to traffic your own ductility, your own total *disposability*, you know?"

"I don't do it," I'm howling. "It's Alix, it's Maron. Alix and Maron do polyamory! It's possibly with Carbon now, I don't know..."

Catching such outlaws of vows, of marital ought-tos, all this *should* stuff — it was Mari's work. It's so out of fashion now. Why wouldn't you simply start contracts — sharing docs, fuck lists — about what you want? What do you want, you want variants? No human, now, calls a *spy* to burst in on conjoining, nothing's sly now, ugh.

Mari's out of work.

Mari says, "I could link polyamory with a vivification of gay and/or Sapphic forms of lust, or inclinations anyway against old controlling customs — this appraisal, this poor study of toxic masculinity — of owning, of holding back, or dominating anybody, but I think it's just, Cu, it's our disposability *only*, it's a dark night of subjugation."

Who would appoint a spy now? Only pry your connubiality into flux, so long as you morally twist into a virtuous slut, is that right?

No doubt about why Mari had to join this cult — a cult! — no spy work for him, no tasks, it's all out of fashion — "But Mari is your gun still . . . ?"

"It's a form of infirmity, Cumin. This libidinous infirmity of any poor old vassal! That old rightwing has its fascism, a significant boon I would say — and our opposing radicalism? Our radical politics? You'll find radicals clutching at, glossing upon — know-it-alls, big shots, *hubristicists* — a list of polyamorous protocols. Smug. Vainglorious.

"What do you all do, Cumin? You all carry out — and turn carnal — your own chains."

"Mari, I'm not polyamorous. I'm looking for a monogamous situation, I'm still hoping."

Mari said I could work on my writing in his mansion's attic, as his captain — old vocal instructor — is out cold past lunch. "Go up and down from this door."

For as long as I wish. It's not a must to join his cult. Or absorb Borax.

An attic this old, Victorian, has a rock wall with mica in it, a starry pulp. And moss, a churchy fuzz worn thin in its misty junctions.

And a fuck chair.

Its dildo is firm and curvy on a ramp on its lap. This is an old chair from a child's room, small, with rocking function. You'd squat lowly onto it.

"With polyamory, a hard and actual inquiry, Cumin, is: *How do you trap a population into working against its own aims?* Capital is nothing if it hasn't a total grasp on you in that downright spot, that distinct habitat or joint of thinking you totally thwart it."

"Mari what is this?"

"A fuck chair."

"For moi?"

"For you, Cu! I thought you'd want it. This stickum stain? I can't post it."

His cult is making fuck chairs for Amazon, all out of gigs, its adjuncts out of class, and so morally sourcing chairs from stray childhoods around, local yard bazaars, and molding dildos off Captain's cock, using only most moral plastics. It's a hit. But Captain — his dick copyright — hoards most gains.

"Thanks, Mari. Truly. I'll try it out. Thanks."

"If your brain injury would only uplift your writing, Cu — you'd cash in."

"What?"

"If brain injury turns into a good way to draft, to soup up manuscripts — this lab is gonna cash in, don't you grasp it? Your work is proof it works. Don't you know how much you count? What you cost?"

"Humans *would* pay to *pay* for brain injury, particularly aspiring authors..."

"Do it, Cu. Producing a book out of this, with all constraints in motion, would bring about such a big OuLiPo boom in popular doctoring, I'm talking major cash flow for Moody — for all of us! A popular aciurgy. All you'd do is ask, at your visit, your ophthalmologist about it."

"But I can't."

"Try!" Mari says, sounding so, so poor. Out of cash.

Mari fucks off. Mari says — I ask — that his cult's cats only *blossom* in a ship's bottom, saprophytic and happy, so don't worry, and I squat onto my own custom-fit, craft fuck chair trying it out, why wouldn't I, wanting many orgasms always if not writing — that's typical — and why not watch mica gloat that it's gold that's in rocks?

You sit on a fuck chair with forthright animus! You fuck its dildo in opprobrium of community. Opprobrium of community is orgiastic. Mari's only downstairs dabbing Borax on his gums, only undoing all doors, only snuggling up to a bunch of cats that flourish without aid of light, gothic cats, parasitic with soil, organics, with scraps, I don't know, is a cat, is cat shit hollow? Is it oil?

This fuck chair is a-rocking as I mount it facing — my boobs smashing through — its back, its dildo maroon, no plum no, burgundy, no, rust but it's so smooth. Mica oinks.

Oh no...

This particular chair, it's too crafty, it isn't vibratory. It's basic. I suck on a chair part, it's wood hints a cacao, old floors, straw and an ivy wall. Look at ivy on a wall for hours! You'll find a mural of story, and story, and story. I don't orgasm without thought — a story. Who can! What woman?

I think about Alix a lot. A lot!

I would fuck him in front of Maron. I would fuck him against Carbon, in a balloon, his bf at work or watching us. Polyamory is a way to fuck a dick. Polyamory is only — I'd say to Mari — pragmatic if what you want isn't good. If you act as this woman wanting a man you don't want a good world. But it's good to fuck (with condonation!) if it's good *or* bad. Polyamory hacks this notion. A fuck chair is a good way, though, I know it, to go off, to fuck off, and that's good, too. If I can work in obscurity, unfound in an old attic with a fuck chair in it, and no Nazis pop in, and mica informs, it's not bad.

I think of Alix. I pour him into my fuck chair story. You know how it is.

I pray to stop crushing, living and subsisting in subordination to my imagination of his big dick and thus dispatching my thoughts to him all night, my rapport by thingamabob — this constant contact with wholly no antiphon. Zip.

Alix, who only would say to Maron (I could hark it past Ruxpin): "Don't worry about Cumin, a third class paranoid bitch."

"Your Android, though" — it's Maron — "is always blowing up, why is that? Back-burning Cumin much?"

"I'll turn it off, I'm not back-burning Cumin, I want to stay in South Philly, not go back to Fishtown, ixnay on my oy-f-bay, I want to turn Cumin's room into our joint printing station" — my aorta sinks.

Alix with no *e* — ugh, how ambrosial.

I still want to gift Moody, his lab, my Oulipian (by brain injury) product, for cash, wanting to dragoon hard coin, incurring wads of cash in this city of hospitals, of cash — wait and mark this, you wait and mark — but I'm still finding it too difficult. No "e," though, is nothing much for writing, fuck. Think of Frank's limitations, for writing if for living, what a primordial, a black swan Oulipian — no *e* is just, it's fucking nothing.

Why Would There Be a Uterus

I LUNCH AT A G-TOWN PUB AND CLIMB BACK UP A BACK stair avoiding a cult run-in. A calico cat, saprophytic, drips up my stairs — a cat in a room is ignition — and start writing Shusaku's book plagiarizing it at will, about cutting up humans a-Hippocratically during World War II but I airlift out *uterus*, so no *u, t, e, r, u* again, or *s* — now *that's* hard.

> An old man will blow in, donning a doc gown. A cop, a cop, add a cop. Old Man will block a jamb facing a fawn of a doc, a boy doc, who will cock on a wall on a nick of bawling. Boy doc will join in now. In back of Boy: an inflow of law; a cop will look on a man — a POW — laying facing a doc and will haw.
> "Go on. Look." A doc will ha-ha oddly. "A cop can blandly know a body, no?"
> A cop will look, a cop having a pygmy lip-do, and now aiming on winning ply, will flap, "Can I film?"
> "Plainly, plainly. I will film, all will. A doc of a high bay will join holding an achingly good Kodak."
> "And now?" Knocking in, a poddy cop will fix on a cap, on a bald conk. "Will a doc hack a conk now?"
> "No, no conk hacking now. In a day."
> "Now a doc pack will only do a biologic bag, an — how do I flap?"
> "I'll coach all. A campaign on a POW, now, will allay any fog — a campaign on knowing if *I* can nick a bag in a man, and how long can I chip, lop off, and hack a bag? How long can I hack a man by a biobag and lacking a final blow? I will now hack away a bag and a half in a man."

It was so difficult writing without a uterus postlunch, damn, not odds-on in my attic toiling, not at all, hiding from a cult and toiling so, taking fuck chair smokos, but so trying to copy out this important part about blood's color jacking up too much, so much it brings on my fainting —

> A bag had a jab. Old Man will lop a pallid caging by a biobag, will hack a biologic bag-caging by hacking gizmo. Old Man will blackly blab, hacking on. Biology will balloon foxily. Foxy blood making foxy, foxy, foxy blood.

God it was so hard! It was so difficult! I had to stop. Uck! A uterus is too glorious, it's important, I can't do much writing without a uterus in our ABCs but I'm noticing — wow — how simplistic, how unfoggy I find it *instantly* to gain it again (still no *e* though ...).

Wow.

What a gift, it's back. I got it back!

I'm in my Frankish attic without much stuff, without *e* still, uck, viva OuLiPo, or Alix, no, and Mari is just nuts (and wouldn't go to my doctor visits) but I admit it's just a picnic now, with morbunditic links to boot, yum, now with *uterus* back in play — joy! — as if a uterus, it wasn't in a scam.

All I'm saying is "no e," in comparison to "no uterus," is fucking *nothing* and, You know what?

It's night.

Mica oinks in stones in G-town. A cat. A foxy cat.

I begin giving myself back not only *u*, *t*, *r* and *s*, I can do it — *e*, as well. I give *e* back to me effortlessly even — still braless, 41 now — and I turn on a light, so what if I get caught? So what! I already know intimately the total feel of Captain's big dick, and it's a good one, so so what? I sit up straight.

My conk is held high.

I oink at the black window, it's fun, looking onto Germantown, its forts and bricks, moss, my upbringing.

Every *e* returns to me suddenly tonight, clauses pop out, yes it's shocking after years of this shit with my brain but suddenness sometimes belongs to you. There is immaterial return. I'm taking it.

Acknowledgments

For the whistleblowers and the testifiers, in every form.
For Jean-Paul.
Thank you to Priscilla Posada, Jeffrey Yang and everyone at New Directions, the Rietlanden Women's Office (Johanna Ehde & Elisabeth Rafstedt), Amina Cain, Jeff Ott, and the Massachusetts College of Liberal Arts and Case Western Reserve University who have supported my working on this one.

Invaluable resources include: the investigative work of journalists Jason Marks, Kevin Romm, and Adrienne Mayfield for WAVY.com and their ten-part series on the crimes of ~~Dr.~~ Javaid Perwaiz; everyone who told me (or the world) things that happened; Erin Osmon's biography *Jason Molina: Riding with the Ghost*, and Jeff Ott's *Weapons of Mass Destruction and the Real War on Terror*; lastly, Shusaku Endo's *The Sea and Poison*.

About the author

CAREN BEILIN was born in Philadelphia in 1983. She is the author of the novel *Revenge of the Scapegoat*, which won the Vermont Book Award for Fiction. Her other books are *Blackfishing the IUD*, *Spain*, *The University of Pennsylvania*, and *Americans, Guests, or Us*. She lives in Cleveland + Philly, and teaches at Case Western Reserve University.

New Directions Paperbooks—a partial listing

Adonis, Songs of Mihyar the Damascene
César Aira, Ghosts
   An Episode in the Life of a Landscape Painter
Ryunosuke Akutagawa, Kappa
Will Alexander, Refractive Africa
Osama Alomar, The Teeth of the Comb
Guillaume Apollinaire, Selected Writings
Jessica Au, Cold Enough for Snow
Paul Auster, The Red Notebook
Ingeborg Bachmann, Malina
Honoré de Balzac, Colonel Chabert
Djuna Barnes, Nightwood
Charles Baudelaire, The Flowers of Evil*
Bei Dao, City Gate, Open Up
Yevgenia Belorusets, Lucky Breaks
Rafael Bernal, His Name Was Death
Mei-Mei Berssenbrugge, Empathy
Max Blecher, Adventures in Immediate Irreality
Jorge Luis Borges, Labyrinths
   Seven Nights
Coral Bracho, Firefly Under the Tongue*
Kamau Brathwaite, Ancestors
Anne Carson, Glass, Irony & God
   Wrong Norma
Horacio Castellanos Moya, Senselessness
Camilo José Cela, Mazurka for Two Dead Men
Louis-Ferdinand Céline
   Death on the Installment Plan
   Journey to the End of the Night
Inger Christensen, alphabet
Julio Cortázar, Cronopios and Famas
Jonathan Creasy (ed.), Black Mountain Poems
Robert Creeley, If I Were Writing This
H.D., Selected Poems
Guy Davenport, 7 Greeks
Amparo Dávila, The Houseguest
Osamu Dazai, The Flowers of Buffoonery
   No Longer Human
   The Setting Sun
Anne de Marcken
   It Lasts Forever and Then It's Over
Helen DeWitt, The Last Samurai
   Some Trick
José Donoso, The Obscene Bird of Night
Robert Duncan, Selected Poems
Eça de Queirós, The Maias
Juan Emar, Yesterday
William Empson, 7 Types of Ambiguity
Mathias Énard, Compass
Shusaku Endo, Deep River
Jenny Erpenbeck, Go, Went, Gone
   Kairos
Lawrence Ferlinghetti
   A Coney Island of the Mind
Thalia Field, Personhood
F. Scott Fitzgerald, The Crack-Up
Rivka Galchen, Little Labors
Forrest Gander, Be With
Romain Gary, The Kites
Natalia Ginzburg, The Dry Heart
Henry Green, Concluding
Marlen Haushofer, The Wall
Victor Heringer, The Love of Singular Men
Felisberto Hernández, Piano Stories
Hermann Hesse, Siddhartha
Takashi Hiraide, The Guest Cat
Yoel Hoffmann, Moods
Susan Howe, My Emily Dickinson
   Concordance
Bohumil Hrabal, I Served the King of England
Qurratulain Hyder, River of Fire
Sonallah Ibrahim, That Smell
Rachel Ingalls, Mrs. Caliban
Christopher Isherwood, The Berlin Stories
Fleur Jaeggy, Sweet Days of Discipline
Alfred Jarry, Ubu Roi
B.S. Johnson, House Mother Normal
James Joyce, Stephen Hero
Franz Kafka, Amerika: The Man Who Disappeared
Yasunari Kawabata, Dandelions
Mieko Kanai, Mild Vertigo
John Keene, Counternarratives
Kim Hyesoon, Autobiography of Death
Heinrich von Kleist, Michael Kohlhaas
Taeko Kono, Toddler-Hunting
László Krasznahorkai, Satantango
   Seiobo There Below
Ágota Kristóf, The Illiterate
Eka Kurniawan, Beauty Is a Wound
Mme. de Lafayette, The Princess of Clèves
Lautréamont, Maldoror
Siegfried Lenz, The German Lesson
Alexander Lernet-Holenia, Count Luna

Denise Levertov, Selected Poems
Li Po, Selected Poems
Clarice Lispector, An Apprenticeship
  The Hour of the Star
  The Passion According to G. H.
Federico García Lorca, Selected Poems*
Nathaniel Mackey, Splay Anthem
Xavier de Maistre, Voyage Around My Room
Stéphane Mallarmé, Selected Poetry and Prose*
Javier Marías, Your Face Tomorrow (3 volumes)
Bernadette Mayer, Midwinter Day
Carson McCullers, The Member of the Wedding
Fernando Melchor, Hurricane Season
  Paradais
Thomas Merton, New Seeds of Contemplation
  The Way of Chuang Tzu
Henri Michaux, A Barbarian in Asia
Henry Miller, The Colossus of Maroussi
  Big Sur & the Oranges of Hieronymus Bosch
Yukio Mishima, Confessions of a Mask
  Death in Midsummer
Eugenio Montale, Selected Poems*
Vladimir Nabokov, Laughter in the Dark
Pablo Neruda, The Captain's Verses*
  Love Poems*
Charles Olson, Selected Writings
George Oppen, New Collected Poems
Wilfred Owen, Collected Poems
Hiroko Oyamada, The Hole
José Emilio Pacheco, Battles in the Desert
Michael Palmer, Little Elegies for Sister Satan
Nicanor Parra, Antipoems*
Boris Pasternak, Safe Conduct
Octavio Paz, Poems of Octavio Paz
Victor Pelevin, Omon Ra
Fernando Pessoa
  The Complete Works of Alberto Caeiro
Alejandra Pizarnik
  Extracting the Stone of Madness
Robert Plunket, My Search for Warren Harding
Ezra Pound, The Cantos
  New Selected Poems and Translations
Qian Zhongshu, Fortress Besieged
Raymond Queneau, Exercises in Style
Olga Ravn, The Employees
Herbert Read, The Green Child
Kenneth Rexroth, Selected Poems
Keith Ridgway, A Shock
Rainer Maria Rilke
  Poems from the Book of Hours
Arthur Rimbaud, Illuminations*
  A Season in Hell and The Drunken Boat*
Evelio Rosero, The Armies
Fran Ross, Oreo
Joseph Roth, The Emperor's Tomb
Raymond Roussel, Locus Solus
Ihara Saikaku, The Life of an Amorous Woman
Nathalie Sarraute, Tropisms
Jean-Paul Sartre, Nausea
Kathryn Scanlan, Kick the Latch
Delmore Schwartz
  In Dreams Begin Responsibilities
W. G. Sebald, The Emigrants
  The Rings of Saturn
Anne Serre, The Governesses
Patti Smith, Woolgathering
Stevie Smith, Best Poems
  Novel on Yellow Paper
Gary Snyder, Turtle Island
Muriel Spark, The Driver's Seat
  The Public Image
Maria Stepanova, In Memory of Memory
Wislawa Szymborska, How to Start Writing
Antonio Tabucchi, Pereira Maintains
Junichiro Tanizaki, The Maids
Yoko Tawada, The Emissary
  Scattered All over the Earth
Dylan Thomas, A Child's Christmas in Wales
  Collected Poems
Thuan, Chinatown
Rosemary Tonks, The Bloater
Tomas Tranströmer, The Great Enigma
Leonid Tsypkin, Summer in Baden-Baden
Tu Fu, Selected Poems
Elio Vittorini, Conversations in Sicily
Rosmarie Waldrop, The Nick of Time
Robert Walser, The Tanners
Eliot Weinberger, An Elemental Thing
  Nineteen Ways of Looking at Wang Wei
Nathanael West, The Day of the Locust
  Miss Lonelyhearts
Tennessee Williams, The Glass Menagerie
  A Streetcar Named Desire
William Carlos Williams, Selected Poems
Alexis Wright, Praiseworthy
Louis Zukofsky, "A"

*BILINGUAL EDITION

For a complete listing, request a free catalog from New Directions, 80 8th Avenue, New York, NY 10011 or visit us online at **ndbooks.com**